The Judas Hunters

By the same author

Lawful Assassins
The Outcasts
Mission to Kill

The Judas Hunters

JAMES O. LOWES

A Black Horse Western

ROBERT HALE · LONDON

© James O. Lowes 2000
First published in Great Britain 2000

ISBN 0 7090 6662 7

Robert Hale Limited
Clerkenwell House
Clerkenwell Green
London EC1R 0HT

The right of James O. Lowes to be identified as
author of this work has been asserted by him
in accordance with the Copyright, Designs and
Patents Act 1988.

Typeset by
Derek Doyle & Associates, Liverpool.
Printed and bound in Great Britain by
WBC Book Manufacturers Limited, Bridgend.

ONE

'Find the Judas and kill him!' The words were spat like bullets and the president sitting behind his desk leaned forward; his scrawny neck and head above the black-coated shoulders reminded General Fothergill of a great black crow. His eyes blazed.

'But Mr President, we have no real proof that Colonel Waterford is still alive! After all, we only have the dubious testimony of a hysterical drummer boy and a private who is a well-known drunk and could have been hallucinating!'

The president tapped his desk with impatient fingers.

'But they were the only two witnesses left alive! A whole damn company massacred! Deliberately betrayed to the Rebs by their own commander! It's dishonouring the good name of the Union Army! It's more than an outrage! It's ... it's....' The President choked in his fury. 'His body was never found with his aides! Good God, even I can deduce what happened! He was bribed and the bastard is now living it up in the south. He must be!' The president banged his desk with his fist. 'I want him dead!'

General Fothergill licked his lips. It wasn't often the president whipped himself into such a rage, then Fothergill remembered that the president's nephew had been one of Waterford's aides and his body had been shot to hell by Rebel gunfire.

The battle of Black Horse Creek outside Richmond had nearly turned the war to the Confederate's favour and it had only been General Ulysses S. Grant's shrewd choice of commanders that had halted the rallying of the Rebel forces.

The battle of Black Horse Creek had remained a shameful episode in the annals of that war and though the testimony of the Fourth Cavalry, who'd gone too late to the assistance of Waterford's cavalry, had aired their doubts after looking on the field of battle, seeing the dead men and horses lying in groups, nothing had been done until the two survivors who'd been classed as deserters had been caught and brought to trial. Then the whole miserable story had come out.

Both man and boy, interrogated at different times, had told the same story. That Colonel Waterford had issued orders to Captain Pearson to charge instead of forting up. That he himself had stayed behind and watched on a hilltop while the men rode into the trap set by the Rebels.

The drummer boy, only fifteen years old, had panicked. He'd thrown away his drum and hidden in a clump of rocks but he'd watched the massacre, being violently sick and had then seen the colonel turn his horse and ride away alone in a southerly direction.

Sam Small, already drunk before the action, told a similar tale and would not alter his statement. The colonel, he said, and he spat as he spoke, watched his troop follow Captain Pearson's command to charge. He had seen the entire troop gallop straight into the Rebel lines and watched as the big guns bellowed and scattered their lethal shells filled with iron filings. The colonel, Sam testified, showed no distress. He seemed jubilant and when it was all over he turned and rode away south.

'And where were you, Private Small, when this happened?' the white-faced military prosecutor asked.

'Where all my comrades should have been, in a ditch ducking the shells and keeping my head down!'

'Well, General? What do you mean to do about him?'

General Fothergill rasped his chin.

'I could put the Pinkerton Agency on to it. They've got good men to do the detective work. Of

The Judas Hunters

course it will take time. . . .'

The president thumped the desk again.

'Not good enough! This is a military matter. Honour is at stake! I don't want this shameful episode made public! It has to be suppressed. What do you think would happen if the American people knew we'd harboured traitors in our midst? We'd lose credibility and God knows we have plenty of enemies without making more! No, you put that renegade outlaw of yours on his trail. If anyone can catch him, it is Major Wilde and his men. You do that, General. Get in touch with Wilde. He'll know what to do!'

'But, sir, we don't know where to start looking!'

'Don't let that worry you, General. Let Wilde cope with the problem. I want results and I want them fast!'

'But, Sir. . . .'

The president got up from his desk.

'Good day to you, General. I don't want to know the details. All I want from you is to get that Judas, and get him fast!'

TWO

Major Horatio Wilde, known as Sabre Wilde, because of the deep slash puckering his left cheek, studied General Fothergill. The old man had aged since their last meeting. His close involvement with the President seemed to be no sinecure. Worry lined his face. He was a careworn unhappy man.

There had been times when Wilde had cursed him and the President for their arrogance and the power they held over him and his men; power that had changed all their lives.

But the orders they'd been given, from the President himself through Fothergill, had had to be obeyed. Anything else would have been considered treason against the United States of America and also a loss of honour in the Army itself.

He and his chosen men had sacrificed their personal honour for the good of their country. But that sacrifice would never be made public. They lived a lie. They lived to do the President's will.

Sabre Wilde experienced again the thrill of the chase as he listened to General Fothergill's reason for the meeting in the presidential railway coach now idling in a siding outside Washington.

'So, what do you know about this Colonel Waterford?'

General Fothergill opened up his briefcase, brought out a thick wad of papers and pushed them across the table separating them.

'It's all there, from his signing on as a cadet at West Point and his first appointments as a lieutenant and then as captain with the Seventh Cavalry. He left the Seventh under a cloud – gambling debts and seducing his colonel's wife. We pick him up again as a major in one of the Mojave desert forts. A tough disciplinarian, unpopular with his men. When the war came he was transferred to General Beresford's command to lash the raw recruits into shape. It was mostly raw recruits who were massacred at Black Horse Creek. He was made up to colonel on the battlefield. I don't think he had any loyalty to his regiment. He was something of a lone wolf.'

'I understand the President's nephew was one of his aides?'

'Yes, that's why there's all this hoo-ha and why the old man's so bitter. He wants the bastard found and executed.'

General Fothergill always used the term

'execute'. He thought it sounded more respectable. He didn't like the idea of telling a man to go out and deliberately bushwhack a victim without warning. It was too much like murder. To be executed was the right punishment for a crime against the United States of America.

'Mmm, quite a pile of reading, General.'

'Might give you a clue where to start looking for him.'

Sabre Wilde nodded. 'It will give the fellers something to study. George usually comes up with some bright ideas. He can always read between the lines. He's got a wily brain, has George.'

'How is George? As surly as ever?'

Wilde laughed and shrugged. 'Same old George. Grumbles mightily but loyal as they come.'

'And the others? Sergeant Roscoe and the lad he befriended?'

'Young Ned? Oh, Private Skinner will never change. Still a soldier at heart. Always follows Roscoe's lead. The old man is good for him. Keeps his feet on the ground. He's like a father to Ned.'

The general grunted. 'They've got no regrets?'

Sabre Wilde threw him a quick discerning glance. 'Feeling guilty, General? They've got regrets and so have I. It's natural, isn't it? We've sacrificed our family life and our honour with it. It hurt George the most. He lost his fiancée through it and his mother and brother think of him as a renegade, so wouldn't you have regrets if you were he?'

'What about you, Major?'

There was a long silence while Sabre Wilde thought of his own situation. He wasn't aware that he sighed. General Fothergill watched the hard face curiously. The man had changed a lot since those far-off days when Wilde had been singled out as the officer most trustworthy to take on the President's task of becoming his own private man-hunter.

'I get by, General. I try not to think of the past,' he said finally.

'What about the gold bullion?'

'What about it?'

'Look, you were never meant to keep that bullion! It was an excuse for you and your chosen men to step over the line and become outlaws! That bullion belongs to the Treasury. You were supposed to return it and make good the deficiency in the Treasury.'

'You really think that gold would have been returned to the Treasury? Are you that naïve, General?'

'What do you mean, naïve?' the general asked sharply.

Sabre Wilde frowned. 'Or were you in the plot too? Maybe you and the President would have shared that gold.'

'Major Wilde . . .' the general began furiously, but he was chopped off by brusque words from Wilde.

The Judas Hunters

'No need to holler, General. It's feasible. How could the return of the gold be explained? Unless of course you wanted to admit publicly that Sabre Wilde and his men were not outlaws after all. That wouldn't have served. Would it?'

'I don't know what you're talking about!' the general spluttered.

'Look, the way I see things, General, is that me and my men might some day become an embarrassment to the President and then what would happen? We could be hunted down by our own erstwhile comrades and shot!'

'No, never! I'd never allow it!'

'You might not be alive, General! So we keep the gold as an insurance. All my men were present when it was buried. They know that if anything happens to me then those who remain alive share that gold and go their separate ways and make a new life for themselves. Wouldn't you call that fair after all the botheration we go through for the President's benefit?'

The general looked uncomfortable.

'I never really approved of this arrangement, Wilde, but I also saw the need to bring justice to those who betrayed us. The President has many enemies and at the moment the present government is rocky. As you know since Lincoln's assassination there has been a lot of political in-fighting and though the war is over, there is still a secret war being waged between the North and the South. It will be years before these issues are settled.'

'In the meantime you expect me and my men to seek out and destroy all those who have harmed the presidency.'

'You're doing a fine job, boy. The President would like to give you all medals, but of course he can't do that. But you have his grateful thanks.'

'And his grateful contributions to our bank accounts!' Wilde said with some irony.

'Yes, of course,' the general said quickly. 'You will find the accounts are up to date if you care to look them up.'

'Thank you. I know the men are most grateful.'

Sweeping the papers up, Sabre Wilde stuffed them into his shirt. The bulge was hidden by his leather jerkin. He stepped to the open door of the coach and leaning out, waved to the bunch of men on horseback waiting at the rear.

The general heard the thundering of hooves and watched the galloping riders kicking up a dust as they raced to come to a full stop outside the coach.

The general caught a fleeting glimpse of the slim Mexican girl, Carla, with the long flowing black hair that he'd heard about, and the Bronco Apache, Johnny Eagle Eye, riding at her shoulder. He looked exactly the same as he'd done when he'd scouted for the regiment, dirty red sweatband knotted around the forehead and a greasy black Stetson pushed far back on his head, the same medicine bundle hanging around his neck.

He saw too, the freed black slave, Joshua, whom he'd met on an earlier assignment. So he'd stayed with Wilde, the general mused. He shook his head. Wilde was a good leader of men. They needed men like him in the army. It was a pity that to all intents and purposes, Wilde had lost his commission.

For the first time, the general felt real anger at his President. It was a good life thrown away. And for what? Just to preserve the President's prestige and safeguard his interests. He doubted very much whether hounding Colonel Waterford to his death would change anything in Washington.

Perhaps all this was just to feed the President's own self-esteem. Suddenly, General Fothergill wasn't sure of anything any more.

He watched Sabre Wilde leap lightly aboard his horse as George Lucas arrived with Roscoe and young Ned Skinner in the rear.

Sabre Wilde took off his hat and waved. The general waved back. The others cheered him, then they wheeled at an angle, and galloped away from the railway track in a whirl of choking dust.

The general watched until they disappeared over the skyline. Then he gave the order for the train to reverse and return to Washington.

He wondered how long it would be before he got the signal in Washington that the assignment was completed.

One thing was for sure. He would make no mention to the President of Wilde's observation about the gold bullion.

The major had a point. Situations could change. Sabre Wilde the outlaw could become an embarrassment to the Government. Some day someone in office might make a decision to have him eliminated.

He liked Major Horatio Wilde.

If it was in his power, he'd see that the boy kept the gold and that all his men could start new lives well away from Washington and all the goddam pen-pushers.

But was it too late? Was the major he knew gone for good and only Sabre Wilde, the outlaw, left? Time would tell.

The galloping bunch of riders kicked up a small whirlwind of dust as they crossed the sage-dotted prairie. Sabre Wilde led the small group, George Lucas at his shoulder, Roscoe and Ned Skinner close behind. Carla, with hair streaming in the slipstream, led Johnny Eagle Eye and the freed negro slave Joshua brought up the rear.

George Lucas glanced several times at the set weathered face of their leader who showed no emotion but was determined to get as far away from the railway track as possible in the shortest space of time.

At last, when Wilde pulled up to allow the horses a breather, George spoke his mind.

'Good news or bad news, Sabre?'

Wilde gave him a quick glance.

'It's good news for you that there are no women involved. The bad news is that the bastard we're looking for has gone to ground and Fothergill has no idea where we start looking.'

George Lucas stared ahead as he rode at an easy canter.

'Who is it?'

'Colonel Rupert Waterford. I've got all the relevant papers on him. He was with Beresford's command.'

'Hmm. Rupert Waterford. If it's the same Waterford I came up against when I was a lieutenant, the man was a pig. A fanatic on discipline who thought the only way to toughen up new recruits was to half-kill 'em, you know – full packs on parade in the hot sun. Swore it was character-forming. A good percentage of the lads died of exhaustion before they ever fired a gun!'

'Then your New England conscience won't suffer when we go hunting?' George Lucas spat, just missing his horse's mane.

'Not a bit of it! This feller will deserve all he gets! One thing though, do we all get to see his record?'

'Oh, yes. I want all opinions on this one. The two survivors of the troop say he went south but that's all we know.'

'So maybe we should go find those two survivors and have them tag along?'

Sabre Wilde pursed his lips.

'Depends on the men involved. How do we explain why a bunch of outlaws are after a renegade colonel?'

'A private matter? There must be lots of men out there who'd like to slit the bastard's throat!'

'Too true. Maybe it would work. At least we can look 'em over. One was an old man, a regular. The other was just a kid, a drummer, still wet behind the ears. In the deposition it was said the boy lost his folks and stayed with the old man who befriended him. I reckon he should be eighteen or so now. We'll talk it over when we get back to camp.'

It was nearly midnight when the tired bunch moved cautiously through trees and rocks and came upon their hideout amidst the Blue Ridge Mountains. Over the years they had found and maintained hideouts set near Washington and further west into Kansas, the Indian Territory, and Texas. They needed the boltholes and each camp was a small-scale fort with all the dry goods and supplies they would need to last them at least six months.

They relied on hunting for their own fresh meat and Johnny Eagle Eye's expertise in knowing plants and roots to dig for in the forests. They all enjoyed fishing in the shallow fast-flowing rivers when they were between assignments. The only thing they lacked was liquor and women.

The Judas Hunters

Sabre Wilde watched the mood of the men and when tempers flared and too much interest in Carla was manifest, he would give permission for those who wanted to, to take a day's ride into a town far enough away for them to be safe and let off steam. He rarely rode off himself, but he knew it was imperative for the boys to do so.

The reason for this was Carla. She made Sabre feel uncomfortable. She had a fixation for him which he did not return. To him she was a spunky young girl, alone in the world since her folk were dead. She reckoned being rescued by Sabre Wilde and his men now meant they were her family. He couldn't abandon her in some strange town. That would be like throwing her to the wolves. Besides, she was courageous, could shoot like a man and was wild on horseback and never allowed herself to be a drag on them. Once, when she had first joined them, he had threatened to leave her behind if she could not keep up with them. She never ever let that happen. He regarded her as a useful member of the team.

But she was a woman.

George Lucas was very aware of the fact and she wanted none of him. It was ironic. She lusted after Sabre Wilde and George Lucas lusted after her. Also in a quiet way did the rest of the red-blooded men except Johnny Eagle Eye who liked mature Indian squaws with big tits and bottoms.

So there was every excuse for the men's frustrated feelings to run high when Carla moved gracefully about the camp doing her chores during those periods of enforced rest.

A signal from General Fothergill with orders from the President was usually met with both foreboding and excitement. They could all let off steam and all petty frustrations were forgotten. They smelled blood like hounds on the scent. They were keen and eager to do their duty.

Gradually over time, they had all subtly changed. Their first forebodings at their new life were feelings of the past. They had got used to the excitement, and the freedom to come and go as they liked was fast turning them into cold-blooded killers. After all, wasn't that what the President of the United States wanted?

Only George Lucas held on to his aversion of hunting down female traitors. He still could not stomach the ultimate killing of a woman in cold blood.

Sabre Wilde was beginning to become aware of change and strove to control the savagery just under the surface of them all, even himself. Sometimes he lay awake at night, wondering how it would all end. If anything should happen to President Johnson, would they be hounded and killed one by one until there were no witnesses left to tell the true story of these turbulent years that beset the government after the horrendous war between the North and the South?

In camp he looked at them all gravely as Carla and Joshua busied themselves in building a fire and cooking a meal that they all needed.

'George here seems to be the only one to know anything about Colonel Waterford, and what he knows isn't good. I want you all to read and study the file on this man and if any of you have any ideas, please air them. We're all in this together. How do we start looking for him?'

There were grunts as they divided out the file of papers between them. They scanned them over by the light of the camp-fire. Sabre stood up and stretched. He was tired and stiff from hours of riding hard. He would check over the horses as the men studied the sheets.

He was worried about his favourite gelding. He'd begun to limp a little during the last few miles. He'd have to doctor the beast before they set out on the hunt.

Johnny Eagle Eye joined him as he was examining the front foreleg. He'd found a stone wedged between the hoof and the shoe. It would have to be removed. He was gripping the hoof between his knees when Johnny apppeared.

'There's been someone here,' he began abruptly. Sabre Wilde's head snapped up.

'When?'

'Within the last two days.'

'Did they find our stores?'

'No. Strange tracks, one ridden horse and a

heavily laden mule rode around the perimeter of the corral. Then they were hitched behind the rocks yonder and the feller spent some time watching the cabin. There's boot tracks where he walked up and down, all jumbled up, and a couple of stamped-on cheroots. It didn't look as if he was trying to hide, just being careful.'

'A prospector, would you say?'

'Could be, or someone lost. D'you want me to scout around and find him? It'd take a coupla days.'

Sabre shook his head. 'No time for that. We must be on our way to hunt up this Waterford feller.'

'What if this stranger cottons on to what he found and brings back a posse?'

'We'll have to take the risk. We'll be long gone before he gets back.'

'What about the stores?'

'He didn't get near the stores, did he? No trace of him mooching around?'

Johnny shook his head. 'The boulder to the cave wasn't moved. There were only the tracks of a mountain cat and its droppings around.'

'Good. So if anyone comes snooping, they'll not find much.'

'What about this white renegade chief? This Waterford?'

'Colonel Waterford. Ordered his men into battle and got all his men massacred but two. They both say it was deliberate and that the bastard rode south immediately after.'

'So we find the two men and talk to them?'

'That's the idea, Johnny.'

'So where are we heading for, boss?'

'Texas. We gotta find Sam Small and that young kid. They're mentioned in the deposition as now living somewhere in the region of San Antonio.'

Johnny whistled. 'Some ride, boss. We'll all have blisters on our arses. What about Carla?'

'What about her?'

'She'll not take kindly to being left behind. But it's a long undertaking for a squaw.'

'She's not a squaw, Johnny. She's a member of the team.'

Johnny lifted his shoulders in disapproval.

'She's female. She'll hold us back.'

Sabre looked hard at him but his bronze face showed no emotion. It was like carved teak.

'We'll put it to her. She can stay behind and guard this place or come with us.'

'If she stays here, she might be bushwhcked.'

Sabre sighed. 'What you reckon we should do with her then?'

'Leave her at the first mission we come to!'

Sabre gave him a sidelong glance. 'You don't much like Carla, do you?'

Johnny shrugged. 'She make big trouble. Too . . .' he shrugged again, 'too macho. Not all woman like Indian squaw. Fight too well with temper to match!'

Sabre grinned. 'I really believe you would like her in your tepee!'

Johnny's usual carved teak face twisted as if in pain and his glance was reproachful.

'Never! I like a woman with meat on her bones!'

'But you must admit that Carla has never let us down!'

'True. But there is always a first time!'

Sabre shook his head He finished looking over his horse's feet and then proceeded to examine the other animals. It was vital for their chances between life and death to have horses in tiptop condition and Sabre always checked them himself.

There was a good smell of venison stewing over the camp-fire when finally they returned. Joshua was stoking the flames, his black face glistening with sweat. He was humming one of his strange voodoo songs quietly as he did so. Carla was hacking up lumps of stale bread to dip into the stew when it was ready. Sabre felt his guts rumble and it wasn't just because he was hungry.

'Carla,' he said, plunging in without any preliminary softening up. 'We think it's best if you don't come with us on this expedition. It's going to be a long haul for a woman. . . .' His voice tailed away at the expression on her face.

She threw a baleful glance at Johnny and scowled.

'He's persuaded you, hasn't he?' With that she suddenly raised her arm and the knife she was using suddenly turned into an upturning spinning lethal weapon. It missed Johnny's head by inches as he ducked, and thunked into a tree-trunk several yards away where it quivered, biting deeply into the wood.

There was an appalled silence. Roscoe and Ned Skinner were lounging round the fire cleaning their tack and George Lucas was checking guns and ammunition. They all stopped their labours and stared.

'Carla!' Sabre roared and leapt towards her but Johnny stood unruffled.

'Leave her boss,' he said as Sabre's hands grabbed Carla to shake her. 'If she'd really wanted to kill me she wouldn't have missed!' He walked to the fire and held his hands to the blaze. Joshua, whose eyes had shown their whites suddenly grinned and silently offered him his whiskey flask. Alone of all the group, except for Sabre Wilde himself, Joshua was Johnny's friend.

Johnny's first loyalty was to Sabre, who'd saved his life in the Mojave Desert, but it was to Joshua that he would always turn when he needed back-up or a confidante. They had much in common. More important, they had saved each other's life on occasion and they regarded each other as blood brothers.

Johnny took a swig from the flask and handed it back. His eyes saying their thanks. Only Joshua realized how Johnny was shaken.

'I won't be left behind!' Carla was screaming. 'That pig there is a fool! I can shoot as well as any of you!'

'True . . .' Sabre began, but her rage smothered whatever he was going to say.

'I've always kept up, haven't I? I've proved myself over and over again! If I was gonna fail I would have done so at the very beginning! My arse is one big corn. I don't get blisters any more! I'm as much of a man as any of you!' She glared at them all, daring them to contradict her.

George Lucas gulped. She spoke the truth. He wished she didn't. He wished she was just the pretty young Mexican girl whose passions could be channelled into loving him. But those passions were channelled into violence. Only Sabre Wilde could have tamed her into domesticity and he wanted none of her. He sighed. Life could be a bitch. He kept silent as the tirade went on.

Finally Sabre lost patience.

'All right, you wilful stupid bitch! You can come with us and be damned to you!' With that he grabbed her and strode with her to the edge of the small stream running past their camp-site. He braced himself and threw her out into midstream, where she yelled and spluttered while the men relieved their tension by laughing loudly.

Only Johnny didn't laugh. He walked away into the forest with a dignified tread. For him the episode was over. Forgotten.

Carla crawled out of the stream, water dripping from her long black hair. It clung like rats' tails around her. She shook herself like a dog.

She stripped as she strode to the fire, leaving her wet clothes on the ground.

'Bastards!' she spat as she passed. As she reached the log cabin to go and find dry clothes she tossed off the last garment. The staring men saw a glimpse of long smooth white leg and a vague silhouette of lithe torso and uptilted breasts. Then the door slammed behind her.

Old Roscoe gulped while young Ned turned pink and George Lucas's hands balled into fists. Sabre alone was unaffected. He laughed.

'Cock-teasing little bitch! One of these days she'll go too far and she'll get her come-uppance! Now boys, let's eat and then get down to some planning. Joshua, shove your eyes back into your head and dish out the grub. The little lady will be taking her time, no doubt.'

Joshua rattled the tin plates and ladled out stew. Soon they were dunking bread into the gravy and their minds were taken up with filling hungry guts.

Joshua, with one eye on the cabin door, finally

ladled out a plate of stew and went and knocked at the door. There was no answer, so he opened it cautiously and put the steaming plate on a stool just inside, then he closed the door quietly. Sometimes even macho ladies liked to be alone to hide their weakness. He understood even if the others didn't. In the old days, when Joshua was a slave, he'd seen many white women's tantrums come and go. It just took a little bit of time and patience.

The following morning found Carla up early clashing pans around, bacon fried in strips and new pan-bread curling at the edges. There was no sign of temper and everyone sighed with relief.

They ate heartily and all took care to be polite and thank her. She took their thanks with dignity and was the first one ready, with bedroll and saddle-bags filled and prepared to move out.

Sabre felt a little shame. He should never have doubted her female strength. Johnny joined them from the forest. Sabre never asked where he spent his nights, but it was never in their camp and Sabre respected his customs and beliefs.

He looked them all over. They'd talked late into the night about all the probabilities of what could have happened to the Judas colonel, and all had agreed that the two witnesses must be found and questioned. That was priority.

He saw the cool determination in all their faces. They sat their horses in a line, waiting, mounts twitching and eager to be off. He grinned at them all as he leapt into the saddle.

'Right, boys! Let's get moving! San Antonio, here we come!'

His horse leapt forward and Carla and the rest of them closed in behind him. Soon, the camp was far behind them and only a hazy dust and the screaming of disturbed birds registered their passing.

THREE

It had taken nearly three weeks of hard riding, and boarding of cattle trucks for themselves and their mounts before they eventually reached San Antonio. The spur lines from the main railtracks were now spreading all over the West. Smoke stacks spilled out soot and smoke and though at first the horses panicked at being herded aboard the cattle wagons, by the trip's end they were resigned to it even though their eyes still showed unease.

The conductor of the train watched curiously as the struggling kicking horses were led from the ramps by the fiercest bunch of ruffians he'd seen in an age. He wouldn't have liked to come up against them in the dark. He could have sworn they were outlaws but they didn't seem alert enough to be on the run. But what intrigued him most was the wild-haired woman with them, who wore a divided leather skirt, checked shirt and pigskin vest and had a hard black Spanish-style hat hung round her neck. Her long boots looked well-worn and she swore as she fought her mount, but the beast was soon soothed as she led him round and round in the marshalling yard.

She was a good-looker, all right, he decided, full of passion. He envied the man who could tame her and take her to bed. . . .

The engine gave a couple of toots, the conductor sprang aboard and the line of trucks slowly moved off.

The horses skittered a little at the noise and then calmed down for the short ride in to San Antonio.

They could smell it – a mile from the town centre. A mixture of spices, cow-shit and horse-manure along with human waste. From a distance the adobe houses made a pretty picture. On nearing the town, the illusion was shattered. Broken tiles, open cesspits and mud, hard-baked by the sun, made up the street leading to a square where two listless shade-trees protected a couple of rough benches. It didn't take much imagination to see what it would be like after a rainstorm: churned-up mud making life difficult for everyone.

A store and a saloon were in the vicinity of the shade-trees and the storekeeper came out to view the strangers as they walked their horses down the street, their eyes taking in everything to be seen. A couple of old men sitting smoking on the

The Judas Hunters

benches sat up straighter and watched, wary and waiting.

Sabre stopped at the rail outside the saloon and dismounted, wrapping his horse's reins around the rough wood. The others followed suit and Sabre smiled to himself as the old men's eyes followed Carla's movements. The visibly relaxed storekeeper casually stepped inside his own emporium, convinced now that a bunch of men with a woman in tow wouldn't be shooting up the town.

Johnny stayed outside while Sabre, with Carla and the rest, went inside for a beer and to ask some questions. Inside the saloon it was cool and dim. It took several seconds for their eyes to adjust. The barman was waiting, a grey dishcloth in his hand on the bar. It hid a sawn-off shotgun just to be on the safe side.

'What'll it be, gentlemen . . . and lady?' He nodded at Carla.

'Beer all round,' Sabre ordered. 'Anywhere we can get a bath?'

The barman turned, busy drawing a huge jug of beer from a wooden keg set atop a rough stool. He nodded.

'Down the street at the Widow Gonzalez' place. Staying long, mister, or just passing through?'

Sabre handed the first drawn beer to Carla who took a gulp gratefully. It was cool and sweet. She sighed with relief, her throat had been like sandpaper for the last fifty miles.

'Just long enough to get our bearings,' Sabre answered. 'Heard of a man called Sam Small? There might be a youngster living with him.'

The barman looked at him oddly.

'What you wantin' 'im for? Is he in trouble?'

Sabre laughed, passing along the beers to the waiting men.

'No, nothing like that. We're old buddies. Just looking him up for old times' sake!'

'Seems a long way to come to see him, seein' as he comes from way up north!'

Sabre shrugged. 'As I say, we was riding this way in any case. I take it you *have* heard of him?'

The man shrugged.

'It's no skin off my nose whatever you want him for. Yes, he and the boy have been in here a few times. They're quiet and no trouble. Keep themselves to themselves. They do a bit of ridin' for the QT ranch, but not reg'lar like. They dig ditches and mend fences and such like. The old man has the rheumatiz somethin' bad.'

'Hmm. Where can we find them?'

'Back along the road aways. You come to a turn-off to the left where the trail crosses a patch of sagebrush. You follows the river and their cabin is a bit off the track going to the QT. You can't miss it if you're lookin' for it.'

'Thanks.' Sabre threw him an extra dollar for his trouble.

The man leaned forward. 'You're not gonna hurt

either of 'em?'

'No. As I say, we're old buddies. We just want to talk.'

The barman shook his head. 'They never talked about havin' buddies. They spoke as if all their buddies was dead.'

'Did they now? Now that's a pity. Then we'll have to let them know otherwise, won't we?'

The barman watched as they drank a second round, even the woman kept up with them. He couldn't weigh them up. They looked to be a ruffian bunch except for the woman, but their actions were peaceable enough. It would be interesting to watch for the outcome.

At last they moved out, to the barman's relief. He didn't like strangers coming in bunches. He liked them in ones and twos so's he could keep 'em in control. The sheriff was never about when he was wanted. Always sparkin' the schoolteacher who was supposed to be learning him to cipher.

Sabre asked again for directions to the Widow Gonzales and then they were gone.

Early next morning the barman was swilling out the saloon with water from the horse trough when he saw the whole group walking their horses back along the trail. They looked a little more civilized. They'd had their hair cut and the leader had had his beard trimmed. He could see the distinct cicatrix running down the man's cheek. The barman reckoned it had been done by

The Judas Hunters

a sabre so maybe the men were military men. Could Sam Small and the boy Jodie be deserters? But then the army wouldn't send a posse hunting up a couple of deserters. It was most puzzling.

The air became sweeter as the bunch of men took their time moving along the trail. There was the scent of sage and pine and Carla wasn't the only one to savour the aroma. It was a time of peace for all of them to get the weariness of travel out of tired bones and muscles.

They weren't moving slowly along the trail for no reason. Johnny Eagle Eye was scouting ahead, breaking trail for them as he usually did. Joshua followed behind. This land reminded him of his days as a slave. There had been good times as well as bad ones and he'd enjoyed many a light-hearted scuffle in sagebrush such as this. For a moment he was nostalgic and then thought, what the hell, I'm a free man now and making a new life with folk I think of as family.

Then Johnny was riding towards them, his coppery face impassive. He just pointed behind him and nodded. Sabre spurred his horse and they all followed. Johnny's pinto reared and turned sharply, then they were riding at a brisk canter around a huge boulder, following the track to the left.

They drew up a hundred yards from a small cabin built into the side of a hill. A wisp of smoke curled from a thin metal pipe. A youth was in the act of drawing water from a makeshift well. He stood up, his bucket swinging unheeded from a rope.

Curiously he watched them draw near. It was as if he was paralysed with fright.

Sabre raised a hand and the horses moved forward slowly.

'Ho there, the house! We are looking for Sam Small.'

'Then you've found him. A deep hoarse voice came from the cabin's open door. An army rifle was being held firmly and was pointing at Sabre's heart.

'And what the hell d'you want with Sam Small?' A thin old man stood bow-legged, his grey wispy hair ruffled above keen pale-blue eyes set in a wrinkled well-lived-in face. 'Jodie, get to hell over here and shake your stumps!'

Jodie gave Sabre and the row of silent horsemen a last scared look, his eyes lingering on Carla, before he ran like a frightened rabbit to the cabin.

The old man pointed behind him.

'Get the old shotgun, son, and be prepared to fire it!'

'No need for all that, Sam,' Sabre shouted in a placatory voice. 'We only want to talk to you.'

'What's so important that you've got to bring a posse with you?'

'We happen to ride together, that's all. May we talk to you?'

'What's with the Injun and the black man? I've got nothin' here worth stealin'. We mind our own business, and that's the way we like it.'

'We want to talk about Colonel Waterford.'

Suddenly the rifle wavered and when Jodie returned with the shotgun, the old man put a hand out warningly and lowered his own weapon.

'Hang on, boy. Did you hear, they want to talk about the colonel!' He spat and leaned on the rifle, using it as a walking-stick as if his legs wouldn't support him.

'What you want to know about the colonel?'

'We want to know about that last battle and the massacre and what happened afterwards.'

Sam spat again and cleared his chest. 'He was a bastard, did you know that?'

Sabre inclined his head. 'We've read his file. We've already come to some conclusions.'

'The bastard got away, didn't he? He was never found or punished for what he did.' Now Sam sounded bitter. Then he looked at them all keenly. 'Are you from the army? Are you really lookin' for the son of a bitch?'

'We're looking for him, Sam. You can rest assured on that score. We want him and we want him bad!'

'Then you'd better come in. There's coffee on the stove. I guess you all could drink a cup of coffee?'

The Judas Hunters

He smiled at them all, showing yellow and broken teeth and gaps that looked black.

They dismounted and tied their horses to the small hitching rail and stepped inside the one-room cabin. It had been one of QT's line cabins for the use of the cowboys overnight when they were rounding up cattle or mending fences. It was primitive indeed and it smelled of stale sweat, leather horse-harness and woodsmoke. Carla wrinkled her nose, took her coffee outside and hunkered down with her back to the rough plank wall. She was glad of the respite but would never have confessed her feminine weakness.

Sabre sipped coffee which was surprisingly good and there was sugar in it.

'So what do you know about the colonel? How long did you serve under him?'

Sam spat again on the dirt floor and rubbed it in with the toe of his boot.

'Five . . . six years. Was his batman for awhile until I got shot in the thigh. After that I looked after his horses. He was particular about them. Had a horse called Bluey, a bastard to ride and an unholy devil to shoe. I got many a kick from him. Sam rubbed a hand down his bad leg as if remembering.

'What can you tell us about the colonel himself? Did he have many visitors?'

The old man stroked his grey-bristled jaw reflectively.

'Now and again. Of course there were the dispatch riders with orders and such and the scouts kept comin' in with reports. All the usual stuff. But every so often there would be a rider come in who'd ridden hard and fast and I had to fodder his horse and rub it down. Fair blown the horse would be and, I thought, the son of a bitch'll kill a good horse one of these days. The peculiar thing was that this feller rode off without stopping to eat and the poor bloody horse hadn't had time to cool off. He was a madman, that one was.'

'Did you ever hear what went on between them?'

'Nope. I was too busy tryin' to keep the horse from water. He was fair mad for it and it would have bust his guts if he'd had his fill.'

'So you don't know whether he brought reports by mouth or carried dispatches?'

'Never saw no dispatch bag, just the long-legged bastard throwing reins at me and boundin' into the colonel's tent without waitin' for leave. Anyone else tryin' a stunt like that would have been shot!'

'Did you watch which way he headed when he left?'

'Usually south. I did notice he never used the main trails. He always rode across country, if that's any help.'

'Hmm, it could be.'

Sabre thought for a while and then George Lucas murmured softly,

'What about women, Sam? Did he have a special woman?'

'Funny you should mention that, sir. There was a woman come reg'lar like. She would come at night after Taps. I thought at first she was some old woman and thought it queer. She walked kinda stooped-like, all dressed in black and she kept a black shawl close about her head and face. Then one night I was up tendin' one of the horses and it was a full moon that night. I heard sounds of talkin', for the night was still. I took a peek and saw the colonel and the woman step out of his tent. He took her in his arms and as he did so, her shawl fell off and I saw she was a real beauty. I was so surprised I nearly whistled. You could have knocked me down with a feather!'

'Then what happened?' Sabre was showing signs of impatience as Sam rattled on.

'He walked her a ways past the line of horses and I had to crouch down and hide as they passed. Then I heard the sound of gallopin' hooves and he walked back and the bastard was smilin' like a cat what's got the cream. My skin crawled.'

'Why, Sam?'

'Because it wasn't a kinda lovin' smile, like a feller thinkin' of what happened when he had his leg over. It was a kinda vengeful smile if you get

The Judas Hunters

my drift. It hit me more after the massacre and I wondered whether that bitch had been part of it.'

'How long did this happen before the massacre?'

'Not long. Not a week. Mebbe four days at the most.'

'Would you recognize the woman again?'

'Too true, sir. After all, it's only a little more than three years ago, and I was sure impressed by her. A real looker!'

'Did Jodie know about this?'

'He never saw her but I told him about her. He hated the colonel and couldn't believe the man was human enough to have a woman. Thought of him as the devil himself.'

'Why?'

'Believe me, sir, the whole damn regiment hated his guts! He set punishments far beyond the crimes! He made Jodie beat his drum all night once because he was out of time with the rest of the drummers! He kept everyone awake that night and he himself took off into the forest so that he could have a good night's sleep. Also there were the floggin's, and if he saw a man turn his back during an assault, he shot him down. There were many young raw recruits who died by his hands rather than the Rebs'!'

'So you wouldn't say no if I asked you to come looking for him with us?' asked Sabre softly.

Old Sam's eyes took on a hard piercing gleam.

The Judas Hunters

He looked Sabre straight in the eyes, noting the determined dedication.

'Just who are you fellers? And what would happen to Colonel Waterford if you found him?'

There was a profound silence and Sam nodded his head.

'If you didn't know him,' Sam said slowly, 'and it's takin' all you men to hunt him up, then by all the shades of Hell someone very important is settin' you orders! You're gonna kill him, aren't you?'

Sabre nodded while George Lucas looked away and Roscoe and young Skinner sat staring stonily into the flames of the fire.

Sam Small laughed.

'I'd sure like to see the bastard staked out somewhere on an anthill and watch him suffer! Yeh, I'll come with you if I can bring the boy?'

'Yes, why not?' Sabre breathed easily. The boy was a witness too. Now they might smell blood and get on the Judas trail.

'Any ideas of where he would make for? South?'

'I was once helpin' out in the mess tent when I was recoverin' from my leg wound. He was havin' a confab with his officers about orders from General Beresford, a feller he didn't rate very highly. They'd eaten and drunk well and the colonel bein' a loud-mouth after a bottle or two talked about a place he called Paradise in Mexico.

He'd lived there as a boy. Mebbe there was Mexican in him, he was dark enough. Said he would go back there when he'd made his fortune and spend his old age in luxury.

'The officers laughed and said that if his gamblin' luck didn't change, he'd never go back.'

'So you think he might have crossed the Rio Grande and gone to ground in somewhere he called Paradise?'

'That's the only place I can think of, sir.'

'Don't call me sir. Call me Sabre. You're one of us now.'

Sam Small grinned at them all.

'Well, how d'you know? I feel as if I'm in the army again!'

Sabre brought out his hip-flask, leaned over and gave it to Sam.

'Here, have a snort, Sam. You sure are in an army of sorts!'

Jodie, sitting quiet in a corner and listening with all ears now got up and brought out a couple of bottles of a homemade version of mescal, made from the agave plant. It was drunk with care by Sabre, cautiously by George Lucas and enthusiastically by Roscoe and young Ned. Later, as Sabre and George and Sam looked at the supine figures, Jodie amongst them, Sabre grinned.

'It's good for them to relax. From now on, Sam, we take our lives in our hands. I'm warning you now, we're not exactly known for law and order.

The Judas Hunters

We're all wanted by the law and could be shot on sight. We're coyotes, Sam. You understand?'

Sam's jaw dropped.

'You mean . . . you're outlaws?'

'Yep. Does that shock you?'

Sam gulped, his adam's apple bobbing up and down in his scrawny neck.

'I thought you was some bounty hunters or some such.'

'Nope. Not bounty hunters. Killers!'

Sam was silent for awhile and then looked up slowly at Sabre.

'I'm an old man now and about the end of my rope, but Jodie's different. He's like the son I never had. I wouldn't want anything to happen to him and I don't want him endin' his days shot in the back as an outlaw! He's worth more than that! What happens to us after we find the colonel . . . if we find him?'

'We set you up in any place you want to be. You'll both get enough to buy you a small ranch somewhere and you can start again. I promise that.'

'And if I don't make it, will you look after Jodie?'

'Yes, as I say, on my word of honour, he will be looked after right. Maybe he and young Ned will become partners. I don't propose to keep Ned with me much longer. He needs a break just like Jodie, to start a new life.'

Sam nodded, satisfied.

The Judas Hunters

'Then I don't care what kind of murderin' bastards you are, I would like to see that arrogant son of a bitch sufferin' as he made some of our buddies suffer!'

'We don't go in for torture,' Sabre answered coldly. 'One shot and it's over!'

Sam peered at him respectfully.

'I see you're a man of honour of sorts. Me now, I believe in an eye for an eye and tooth for a tooth!'

'We all have our peculiarities, Sam. Now what about a bit of shut-eye? It's getting late.'

Outside, a small fire was still burning and Carla was curled up in a blanket asleep. Joshua sat with his back against the rough stone of the well, his eyes gleaming in the dim light given off by the fire. He stood up as Sabre and George Lucas approached.

'Everything under control, boss?' He looked behind them for Roscoe and Ned. Sabre grinned.

'Yeah, you might say that, Joshua. Roscoe and Ned will have bad heads in the morning.'

Joshua grinned his understanding. 'All quiet out here, boss. Johnny's done his usual thing and is probably sitting up on some crag, watching and communing with those spirits of his.'

'Good. You get some sleep, Joshua. I'll take first watch and George here will take over in three hours.' He looked at Carla curled up, sleeping peacefully. 'She needs all the rest she can get. It's going to be a long haul.'

George looked down at her.

'We could still leave her at some mission.'

'Not on your life, George. She'd follow us and maybe put us all in jeopardy. Better to have her with us than worry about her!'

FOUR

Father Francis Octavius made the sign of the cross above the unconscious Mexican. The man appeared to have passed over but the father's experienced eye detected a flicker of movement in the chest. He looked across the bed to the woman opposite who sat so still, with hands folded, eyes closed and her lips moving slightly. She was dressed in black and already looked like a widow.

'Maria,' he said gently, 'I've done all I can. Call me when the time is right.'

She opened weary eyes and smiled at him as he clambered clumsily to his feet.

'Thank you, Father. Juan would have been grateful for all the help you have been. Bless you, Father.'

Father Francis bowed his head.

'And a blessing on you, my child.' He made the sign of the cross over her bowed head and left the stiflingly hot, stuffy room, ignoring the two sons and a daughter sitting quietly on stools, their backs against the white adobe wall.

Outside in the bright sunshine Father Francis took several deep breaths to cleanse himself of the human smells and the sweet stench of coming death. This was one of the jobs he hated. He enjoyed the weekly sermons, the exhorting of the faithful to beware of Hell's eternal fire and the occasional times he was called on to judge in a dispute. The christenings were the best, when new life burgeoned and helped to make the village strong.

But death? It brought nightmares and guilt. It was as if it was his fault when a parishioner fell ill and died. He tried so hard to repent all his own early carnal sins that he'd committed during his younger days. They lay heavily on him even now, when he'd carved a niche for himself in this place.

Nuevo Cruz. A small village clinging to the mountain-side, its white adobe box-like houses rising in tiers with tiny strips of land worked by the peons and producing a variety of crops of which Father Francis took a tithe for caring for their souls.

The white church, with its steeple rising to heaven like a finger, dominated the village. It had been built, along with the houses, after the great earthquake in 1751. The cross on the church spire gave the village its new name, Nuevo Cruz, and from then on the village had expanded and improved until it had reached its present prosperity.

Father Francis sighed with satisfaction as he looked down into Nuevo Cruz from Juan Garcia's house. He thanked everything he believed in that he had found shelter in this place away from the hurly-burly of a more modern way of life. He felt safe and secure. This was his niche and, God willing, he would serve this community in the best way he could.

He frowned when he saw a bunch of strangers walking their horses along the wide street. One man rode ahead, with two men close behind and four riders strung out across the street behind them. He squinted against the sun and if his eyes didn't deceive him he saw a glimpse of a black man and an Apache Indian wearing a greasy black army-scout's hat. All had their rifles across their horses' pommels.

Father Francis's heart quickened. Were these men looking for someone in the village? Or were they bank-robbers? If they were, they were going to be disappointed. There was no bank in Nuevo Cruz and the one store only sold staples that the villagers couldn't grow for themselves.

He pulled his own black hat well down over his eyes and walked, with head down, swiftly along the street, his rosary swinging from his waist. His hands he tucked into the sleeves of his black habit. As he walked, he prayed. He wanted no violence in this most serene and pretty village.

He raised his eyes when at last he was within speaking distance and the men had come to a full stop. He raised one arm in a blessing.

'Peace be with you all,' he intoned. 'Can I help you in any way?'

Sabre Wilde studied the priest, noting the heavy black beard, the piercing eyes under the cover of the wide-brimmed hat.

'Is there anywhere we can put up for a few days around here?'

Silently the father pointed further along the street.

'The hostelry is down there and the saloon next door. The food is plain but good. May I ask your business in Nuevo Cruz?'

'You may ask, Father, but you won't get any answers!' With a laugh Sabre turned to those behind him.

'We're in luck, boys. The good father recommends the saloon.'

As they all rode past him the father saw that one of the riders was a woman. He was so surprised that he did not look at the rest of them except for a passing glance at the negro and the Apache.

There was something about the Apache that raised a fleeting memory in him but it was wispy and then gone from his consciousness. He

The Judas Hunters

dismissed it as all Indians looking alike.

Father Francis went on his way. He was a little late in visiting the small schoolhouse where he took prayers each morning. He hurried. He needed to talk to Anita Juarez, the young schoolma'am. She needed to tighten up discipline. Some of the bigger boys had been raiding Lucio's melon patch and it had to stop, or he, the priest, would not get his quota when they were harvested.

The riders dismounted outside the saloon, tying their mounts to the hitching rail and strode into the dim interior where it was cool and smelling of stale beer and last night's sweat.

The barman looked up with bulging eyes, his hand automatically swiping the bartop with a dirty dish-rag. It wasn't usual to get a bunch of strangers coming in together. The village was off the beaten track.

He glanced at the few regulars who played cards. They were the village elders and past working their allotments. They drank sparingly and smoked rank tobacco and passed their days reminiscing about the past. They too stared at the incoming men, forgetting their cards.

Sabre and his party caused a sensation.

'Beers all round, *señor*.' Sabre pulled out a roll of bills, peeled off a couple and placed them on the bar top. 'There's enough there for the boys to drink their fill.'

The barman's eyes bulged at the roll. He looked

at Sabre with respect if not liking. The scar on Sabre's cheek gave him the look of a ruffian.

'*Si, señor.*' Julio began to fill beer jugs and to place earthernware tankards in a row on the bar top. He was breaking out in a sweat and he knew fear was rising in him. Mother of God, he prayed, don't let these men break up my saloon! It took me years of toil and hard work to get the place put to rights after the last gang broke the place up, and what for? Just for the fun of it. Oh, Lady, Mother of God, don't let it happen again!

His hands trembled as he pushed the slopping jugs across the counter.

'There you are, *señor*s, and there's plenty more where that came from!' His mouth opened to show white teeth in a rictus smile but his eyes were frightened.

'*Gracias, señor,*' Sabre poured beer for Carla, the others crowded round and helped themselves.

They sat down at two rickety tables. The barman watched as they laughed and talked together. His attention focused on Carla. A fine-spirited *señorita* who would certainly cause havoc in Nuevo Cruz if she lived here, he thought enviously, his own juices beginning to flow. He wondered whose woman she was; it was probably the good-looking man with the moody face, or maybe one of the young bloods. Both were macho and any woman's dream.

He found himself relaxing. Maybe his prayer

The Judas Hunters

would be answered. Maybe they weren't out to cause mayhem.

Suddenly Sabre turned to him.

'Is there a village around here called Paradise?'

The barman stared and considered, shaking his head, pausing in polishing a tot glass.

'Not in the foothills. Maybe further up in the mountains. There's a place called Paradisio on the other side of the Blue Hills. Maybe that's the place you want?'

Sabre nodded. 'Do you know anything about this place?'

The barman shook his head. 'A dirty township as far as I know. A cattle centre, stinks to high heaven, so a traveller once told me.'

'Doesn't sound like the place we're looking for.' Sabre turned back to the others.

'We might have to do a bit of scouting around.' He looked across at Johnny and Joshua, sat with Jodie and Ned. 'What about you four taking a look-see while we arrange beds for the night?'

Ned drank up his beer immediately and the others followed suit.

'Will do, boss. We'll quarter the surrounding district and ask around and we'll be back after sundown.'

The barman watched the men leave. It must be mighty important to find this place called Paradise. He also wondered what there was in Paradise to be so important.

The Judas Hunters

But there were more urgent matters to be taken care of.

'You mentioned beds, *señor*?' The barman's eyes gleamed. He wondered how much he could take these rich ruffians for.

'*Si*, can you fix us up with three double rooms and two singles?'

'I can with the help of my brother-in-law next door,' replied the barman, thinking to himself that he could make a few cents out of the transaction with his brother-in-law. It wasn't often he could make profit out of that smartarse.

'Good, then if you could rustle up some grub and a bath for us all, we should be grateful.'

Holy mother of God! You've answered my prayer, thought Julio. These men are not violent men, they're just men going about their business.

'I'll see to it right away,' he answered, and he dashed off into the kitchen yelling for his fat wife.

'Conchita, Conchita! Get off your fat arse and prepare food for the *señors*! Quickly, quickly!' He was clapping his hands and the waiting men could hear a furious woman's voice berating her husband for waking her up out of a siesta.

There was much grumbling and the sound of pans being banged about and the smell of hot fat and onions and charring beef. But it was worth waiting for. When the food was ready there were mounds of it, browned steaks, corn on the cob and yams thick with butter – along with blueberry

The Judas Hunters

pancakes with corn syrup for afters and as much strong coffee as they could drink.

Sabre called for the barman's wife when they'd finished. She came shyly, a short, plump woman with a round face and greying hair. She wiped her hands on her apron.

'You like my cooking?'

Sabre belched, which pleased her. She smiled.

'That's what I wanted to tell you, *señora*. Best grub we've had in weeks! Thank you and here's something for yourself.' He shoved ten dollars into her reluctant hand. 'Buy yourself a present from us all!'

She beamed. 'Really? You really mean that?'

'Yes, ma'am. You buy something pretty.'

'Then I'll buy a new rosary. I've only ever had one with wooden beads. I shall buy one with pretty blue stones...'

'Conchita!' her husband yelled at her. 'You don't need a new rosary!' She frowned at him and threw up her hands.

'Mind your own business, Julio! The *señor* said to buy something pretty. I'm buying a new rosary and will get it blessed by the good father!'

'But you know you were complaining about wanting new frying-pans! I thought....'

Sabre stood up from the table, a hard glint in his eyes.

'You heard what the lady said, amigo! I'm paying you the going rate for the meals. Be content with that. What your wife does with her tip is her business. Right?' His face came close to Julio's.

Julio took one step backwards. Suddenly his earlier judgement about these men being non-violent left him. This scar-faced man looked like a killer at this moment. He swallowed. He tried a smile.

'Er . . . right. I was only pointing out that she wanted something more useful. . .' His voice trailed away as Sabre scowled.

'Tomorrow,' Sabre whispered into his ear, 'I want to see that rosary in her hand. You understand me?'

Julio nodded vigorously.

'*Si, si,* señor. You will see it! Would you like more beer?'

'Yes, fill up the tankards again, and tell your wife to have food hot and waiting for our comrades when they return.'

Ned and Jodie arrived together. They looked doleful, shaking their heads at Sabre's enquiry.

'We struck out back towards the Rio Grande, Jodie rode east and I rode west, and we met up in a wide circle. No villages named Paradise or anything sounding like it,' Ned said, wiping dust and sweat from his face. He sat down with a jangle of spurs.

Julio hastily brought both the young men beer to quench their thirst.

The Judas Hunters

'I'll send for my brother-in-law who runs the hostelry to see to your horses,' he said quickly, 'while Conchita brings you some hot food.'

Julio reckoned it was best to keep in with these unpredictable men. He still couldn't make up his mind whether they were sons of the devil or of angels.

'Good,' said Sabre. 'Tell him to give them all extra corn and we'll pay extra, and tell him to look at their feet while he's foddering them.'

Julio skipped away, all nerves, smiling over his shoulder, beads of sweat breaking out of him when he remembered the leader's evil face close up to his. He shuddered. Were they indeed outlaws from north of the Rio Grande?

He badly wanted to know just who they were. Perhaps they were famous outlaws wanted by the *Americanos*. It occurred to him that there might be a fortune on their heads!

If that was so and he was responsible for their capture, then he and Conchita could leave this miserable hole and buy a ranch up in the mountains and breed good horses and fat cattle.

He shook his head. He was only day-dreaming and no good ever came of dreaming.

Joshua came in, sweating and weary. His horse had gone lame. But he too had not found any clue as to where Paradise could be. The locals had looked at him uncomprehendingly. They thought he was mad.

'There just ain't anywhere called Paradise, boss. We're runnin' up a blind alley, boss.' Joshua sank down beside Jodie and sniffed his food. 'I could eat a dead horse without bein' cooked,' he stated and stretched stiffly.

Carla reached for the jug of beer on the bartop and poured some into a clean tankard. It frothed over. She set it before him. He drank deeply after smiling his thanks. Carla was always their ministering angel at any time, whether helping to feed them or binding up their various hurts. Then she was at her best. There was no sign of the virago in her that was always there just under the surface.

She smiled back at him. 'Did you see any sign of Johnny when you were out there?'

Joshua shook his head. 'We split up. He was sure in a hurry. I went one way, he went the other. Seemed to have somethin' on his mind.'

Sabre, hearing the exchange, spoke comfortably.

'We all know Johnny. Comes and goes at will. I don't expect to see him until morning, but I bet my best boots, he'll have something to report.'

And he did.

He came riding slowly down Main Street just after dawn. His pinto's head was down and his flanks were covered in foam. Johnny had ridden hard and fast.

Sabre and the rest of them were enjoying Conchita's pancakes and downing gallons of coffee. They'd all slept well and reckoned this was one good billet.

Sabre raised his head when he heard the measured clip-clop of a tired horse.

'Here comes Johnny if I'm not mistaken,' he declared, swallowing the last of his coffee and belching.

All eyes were on the batwing doors as they creaked open and Johnny paused in the opening. His bronze body was glistening with sweat.

He raised a hand to them all, but his face was grave as he moved a little stiffly to stand before them.

'I found Paradise...' he muttered and suddenly keeled over and slumped to the ground.

For a moment they were all in shock. Then as one man they all made a rush to help him. Sabre turned him over gently and saw the stab wound in his back just above the right kidney. It had bled copiously before drying and his shirt and vest were stiff with dark brown blood.

Sabre swore. Johnny's eyes flickered.

'In the mountains...' Then he relapsed into unconsciousness again.

'He's lost a helluva lot of blood,' Sabre rasped. 'It's a wonder he got here. Someone see to his horse and you Ned, help Jodie to carry him up to my room. Carla, get Conchita to bring up hot water.'

But Carla was already on her way to the

kitchen and was soon upstairs and tearing up clean rags that she'd got from a frightened Conchita.

The wound proved not so deep or serious as had at first appeared. Johnny was suffering more from exhaustion from long hard riding than from the wound itself.

Johnny groaned when he came to and tried to get off the bed when he found he was under a white man's roof. There was nothing Johnny detested more than being too close to white men. If it wasn't for his loyalty to Sabre Wilde, who'd saved his life after he'd been staked out in the Mojave Desert, he would have been long gone, back to the wild freedom of the uncharted wastelands that were still untouched by the invading white men.

Sabre watched Carla as she deftly cleaned and bandaged the wound. She had very capable hands. She should have been a respectable wife and mother by now, not living a precarious existence with such as they, he ruminated. But he knew that she would take badly the first hint of change. She would accuse him of wanting rid of her, and he stayed his tongue. If she left them it would have to be her decision alone. He hoped and prayed that she would never come to harm while they went about the President's business.

Then, when she was finished, he sat on the edge of the narrow bed and watched Johnny who was sweating badly with the exertions of Carla's ministrations.

'Johnny, can you talk?'

Johnny stared at him and nodded.

'You found Paradise?'

'Johnny nodded slowly. 'A hell-hole. Not what . . . you think.' He spoke gaspingly. Speech and movement hurt.

'Did you talk to anyone?'

Johnny shook his head. 'Not a village . . . a ranch . . . watched . . . slaves . . . Indians . . . Mex . . . and some . . . White-eyes . . . not good.' He stopped, panting heavily.

'Take it easy, Johnny,' said Sabre, as Johnny struggled to sit up. 'There's all the time we need.'

'Must get . . . outta here,' Johnny muttered. 'No air . . . stiflin' . . . want . . . outside. . . .'

'All right, Johnny, just as soon as you've rested, we'll leave Nuevo Cruz and camp out in the hills. That do you?'

Johnny nodded and appeared to relax, his eyes shut. Suddenly there issued from his lips the low *Om* sound and his breathing altered. Sabre scratched his beard. He recognized that sound. Johnny was taking charge of his own healing. He'd left them and gone into another dimension. There was nothing to be done.

Sabre glanced up at Carla who understood and nodded quietly. They both left the stuffy hotel room closing the door softly behind them.

Downstairs the others waited, all showing concern for the Bronco Apache who was cast out from his tribe for killing his wife and best friend who'd become her lover. Now, though Johnny preferred his own company to white folk, he was still one of them. They regarded him as family.

'How is he, boss?' Joshua was full of concern. He of all of them was closest to Johnny.

Sabre grinned and they all relaxed. All would be well.

'You know Johnny. Doing his big medicine routine. He'll be up and rarin' to go in a few hours as if nothing's happened.'

'So what did you get out of him?' George Lucas asked. 'He said he'd found Paradise.'

Sabre lit a cheroot before answering.

'It's not a village, it's a ranch and by Johnny's account, there's prisoners up there in the mountains. Johnny calls them slaves.'

'So what are they doing up there?'

Sabre shrugged. 'That's what we've got to find out as soon as Johnny's fit to travel.'

'And in the meantime?'

'We enjoy Conchita's cookin' and heal the blisters on our arses!'

As Sabre predicted, Johnny was up and prowling around the village by early dawn next day. He moved slowly and carefully and studied the ground as he walked to exercise his legs. He found a quiet place just above the village burial ground and greeted the strengthening sun with thanksgiving. He sat cross-legged and contemplated, rocking himself and shaking the small leather medicine bag he carried on a thong around his neck at all times. It rattled. Inside were a couple of bear's teeth along with the skull of a small shrew, a few dried leaves and twigs and spices given to him after his first coup when he turned from boy into man. They were his holy possessions and woe betide anyone if they were ever wrested from him.

He returned, refreshed and ready to ride. He took Conchita's pancakes and coffee and thanked her with grace but carried them outside to the hostelry and squatted with the horses while he ate.

Conchita's eyebrows rose in surprise. 'What's with him? Isn't our saloon good enough for him?'

'Take no notice,' Carla soothed. Even Sam Small and Jodie were nonplussed by the Apache's attitude. 'He don't like white folk around him. Suspicious-like.'

'Then why does he ride with you?' Conchita asked curiously.

'Because he reckons he's blood brother to the boss. Sabre saved his life. He'd die for Sabre.'

'That boss of yours must be some *macho hombre!*'

Carla glowed. 'He sure is! He saved my life. He's a good man!'

'You love him, huh? You his woman?'

Carla's face clouded. 'No. I'm no man's woman!'

Conchita looked surprised. 'You one of those macho he-women?'

Carla looked affronted. She glared. 'No! I love him. He don't love me, so I take no man!'

Conchita shrugged. 'You big fool! Any man better than no man!' She waddled away, laughing quietly.

That night, Sabre allowed the men and Carla to relax and make the most of their free time. Tomorrow would be the beginning of the hunt in earnest for the Judas who had betrayed the men of his command.

They sang folk songs and Carla danced and Sam Small regaled them with Army ballads. The beer flowed and the men of Nuevo Cruz gathered to watch and listen, and later, to join them in the revelry. It was a night to remember and talk about in Nuevo Cruz for many years to come.

Father Francis, attracted by the music from the saloon, looked in, benign and tolerant of his parishioners joining in the fun. His gaze wandered around, noting who amongst his flock were there drinking with the strangers, and came to rest on one particular face. He frowned, then he smiled as if to dismiss his thoughts and lifting a hand he blessed them all before going on his way back to the small church house.

Sam Small stood up drunkenly, belching and swaying.

'Mush go outshide and get shome air,' he hiccuped.

Jodie sprang up to grab him. 'Should I come with you, Sam?'

Sam shook his head vehemently. 'What you think I am? A baby? Want to pish and get shome air. I'll be right back. No shweat!' He lurched outside while Jodie watched him worriedly. He was half of a mind to follow him but knew the old man's temper if Jodie tried to coddle him. He didn't like being helped. He was of an independent nature and help only reminded him he was old and infirm.

Sabre saw the indecision. 'Let him be, Jodie. He'll only get upset if you follow him.'

Jodie sat down and the barman filled up his tankard.

'Here, get that down yer, boy, and let the old man alone!'

Outside, the fresh air made Sam dizzy. He peed against the wall and had difficulty in buttoning himself up again.

'Jesus!' he muttered to himself. 'It was just like the old days in the army mess when we'd sent those Rebs runnin' for their lives!'

He took some deep breaths and decided to walk up Main Street. With a staggering gait he set off, grabbing at hitching rails and walking solemnly around horse-troughs and water-butts. He looked about him. All was still but there were just a few faint yellow lights glowing and flickering from small windows.

It was late but not late enough for all Nuevo Cruz to be sleeping. Except for the few lights, the village could have been dead.

Then a hard hand encircled his neck and he felt the point of a knife digging into his neck just below the right ear. A voice whispered,

'Make a sound and I'll slit your jugular!'

Then he was being hauled into a back lane that joined Main Street at the corner of the grocery store. Sam's heart fluttered. His bowels loosened and he had difficulty controlling himself.

'What you want?' he managed to gasp and choke as the grip tightened about his neck.

The voice in his ear was hoarse and whispery.

'I want to know who your boss is and why you are here?'

The pressure eased a little but the knife dug deeper. Sam coughed.

'We're just passin' through!'

'Liar!' He was shaken like a half-dead puppy. 'You're a Union soldier, ain't you?'

'How d'you know. . . .' The pressure came again and Sam's hands scrabbled at the vicelike grip.

'I know! Just tell me what I want to know!'

'We're lookin' for Paradise!' He heard a gasp behind him. His brain registered that he'd given his assailant a shock.

'Why Paradise?'

The Judas Hunters

Sam was desperate but he also knew his heart was giving out and suddenly he didn't care any more. With the last ounce of courage he had in him he spat out the words his assailant wanted to know.

'We're lookin' for that black-hearted Judas, God's curse on him, Colonel Waterford, may he burn in hell!'

His assailant turned him round savagely and Sam was staring up at the man. His eyes bulged with shock.

'You!' The man's teeth showed white like a ravening wolf's teeth in the fitful light of the moon. 'Yes, you've found him!' With that, the knife sliced into Sam's throat neatly and cleanly and he slumped to the ground.

For a moment the dark figure hovered over him and then he slipped away into the shadows and was gone.

FIVE

Father Francis knelt at the altar with bowed head and hands clasped, his eyes on the two flickering candles before him. His short prayer was finished for the night and he was thinking of the strangers come to the village.

They looked ruffianly and dangerous but by the sounds of revelry still going on in the saloon, the village men were taking full advantage of free drinks.

He had a shrewd idea why the scar-faced leader was being so lavish with his free drinks. He was wanting information from those who could supply it. But what was he after, or rather who was he after?

He ruminated on the evening's events and closed his eyes and said another prayer. It eased his soul somewhat.

Then he heard the church door creak open. He got to his feet and turned to see who would come into the church this late at night.

The Judas Hunters

He saw a muffled dark figure with black hat well pulled down over his face. The flickering candles did not give enough light to see who it might be but it was certainly not one of his congregation.

'Who comes into my church so late at night?' he asked sharply, and watched the dark figure pause and genuflect before walking slowly up the centre aisle towards him.

'You be Father Francis Octavius?'

'I am. What can I do for you?'

The stranger took off his wide-brimmed black hat and stared with hard eyes at the priest. Father Francis felt sudden fear shaft through him as he studied the implacable features of the man before him.

'What is it?' His voice died in his throat.

'It is more what can I do for you!' the answer came in a menacing whisper.

'I don't understand.'

'You will!'

The air in the saloon was thick with smoke. Julio, the barman, was still busy filling tankards. He was smiling broadly now. He'd never had such an evening. He couldn't thank the strangers enough for coming into his saloon and spending so much good *dinero*. Old Antonio was singing and dancing and everyone bellowed the choruses and there were many of them for Antonio's songs always had a lot of verses.

The Judas Hunters

Jodie kept looking around for Sam. It had been a long while since Sam had gone outside for fresh air. Jodie reckoned that the old fool had hunkered down somewhere and passed out. He didn't want to appear to be Sam's minder, for the old man was sensitive about his increasingly stiffening bones.

Finally he could stand it no longer. He must go and see if the old man was all right despite Sam's sure anger at his interference.

Outside, he took several deep breaths of air. He hadn't realized just how hot and stuffy it was in the ramshackle building. The night was still overcast. He looked about him, expecting Sam to be sitting smoking somewhere but all was silent. Main Street was mostly in darkness. No one was on the street and only a few dim lights shone through dirty window-panes.

He walked as far as the store and turned back and walked down towards the hostelry. He paused at the opening of the alley bordering the hostelry. The air smelled of horses and manure and sodden straw.

'Sam? Where are you, Sam?'

His eyes adjusted to the night. He saw the horse trough, in front of the hostelry, and the crosstree that riders used to hang up saddles while attending their horses. He also saw the old buggy in the alley which could be rented out by the hour.

He smiled with relief. That would be where the

The Judas Hunters

old devil was. He must have climbed inside and gone to sleep. He walked towards it quietly, intent on giving Sam the surprise of his life when he fell over an obstacle that had been hidden in shadow.

'Goddammit!' he muttered as he fell and then he felt the chill fingers of fear running up and down his spine as his groping fingers felt the body of a man. A man who was very dead.

He scrambled to his feet, stupidly looking at the sticky mess on his fingers. He knew what it was. It was blood and just beginning to congeal. He staggered back.

'What in hell. . . !' Then he was down on his knees, turning the body over, but he didn't have to do that to know who it was. He knew that jacket anywhere.

'Sam!' The word was a sob in his throat.

Sam lay, still slightly warm, his face waxen white, the grey stubble on his chin taking on a dirty yellow colour. A great gash that looked like obscene red lips was once his throat and his shirt was a welter of crimson blood where he'd bled to death.

Jodie felt faint and nauseated. He took several deep breaths and stood up, careless that he too was bloodied.

'Oh, my God . . .' he gasped aloud. 'I don't believe it!' Then he threw up and collapsed beside Sam. The world heaved and shuddered, then he dragged himself upright and staggered back to the saloon.

He opened the swing doors and lurched inside, his face a ghastly white. He hung on one swinging door as he came to terms with the fact that the old man who'd befriended him and whom he'd come to regard as his father, was dead.

Sabre looked towards the door, conscious of the cold night air rushing in. He put down his tankard sharply, the laughter on his lips dying, as he saw Jodie's face. He sprang up and caught the boy as he stumbled.

'What is it, Jodie? For Christ's sake take a hold of yourself!' He slapped him lightly across one cheek. 'What's happened, boy?'

Jodie flinched at the slap and tears welled in his eyes but he shook his head and straightened up.

'It's Sam. Someone's cut his throat!'

The words resounded around the saloon and the music and singing ceased as a great gasp went up in the air. Then the stunned silence was deafening.

Suddenly everyone spoke at once and George Lucas and Ned Skinner – along with Roscoe, followed Sabre outside while Carla took charge of Jodie. Joshua was already snoring in a corner and it was best to let him sleep. He was apt to go a little loco if awakened unduly.

They found Sam's body in the alley. A quick

examination showed he'd been knifed by a professional. The cut was one clean slice by a right-handed fist.

Sabre stood upright and looked at George Lucas.

'It sure looks as if our Judas is aware he's being hunted!'

'But how?' asked George, puzzled. 'We're the only strangers come into the village.'

'News travels fast. Maybe there's a look-out living in Nuevo Cruz and one of us has been opening his mouth too wide!'

George shook his head.

'None of us has talked out of turn, I could swear my life away on it.' He looked around. 'Anyone been asked some awkward questions?'

The others shook their heads.

'We been all together apart from Johnny, that is. But no one would make him talk,' Roscoe said slowly. 'Could it be that Sam saw someone outside who he recognized? Someone cut his throat to shut him up?'

'Goddammit!' Sabre exploded. 'But there was only him and Jodie left alive after the massacre!'

'What about the colonel himself?'

Roscoe's question had them all transfixed.

George Lucas swore.

'Perhaps this Paradise business was some kind of a blind and he's hiding out somewhere in this region.'

The Judas Hunters

Sabre nodded.

'It figures. Let's go get this barman and find out if there've been other strangers settling down in these parts.'

But Julio was adamant on that score.

'If an *Americano* had come to live amongst us, I surely would have known. We're a small community and everyone knows everyone else. The big *rancheros* around here are all Mexican. Old families well respected. No, *señor*, there is no such man that you look for! You must ask Father Francis and he will tell you the same. He knows everyone for are they not all part of his flock?'

It was early next morning when they found that Johnny had not slept in the barn as had been arranged. He'd slipped away some time during the night to sleep away from the village and under the stars as was his wont.

He arrived back just after daybreak.

His face was inscrutable when he was told of Sam's killing. He showed no surprise or sorrow. Sam's life span had been ordained before birth. It didn't matter to Johnny how Sam made the transition. He was now in his own happy hunting ground. Only if it had been Sabre Wilde who'd been killed would he have danced the death ritual and chanted the mantra for the dead as was fitting, for was not Sabre Wilde his blood brother?

The body had been taken to a run-down stable

with a sagging roof, smelling of damp and mildewed hay. Johnny went to look at and noted the angle of the slash. He nodded slowly.

'It was not a Bowie knife but a curved Indian knife such as the Shoshone use, but used by a white man. A Shoshone would hook and slash.'

'So it was someone who'd come by an Indian knife, maybe taken from an Indian corpse?'

Johnny nodded.

'A white man's habit. To take a weapon as proof of victory as we take scalps!' He walked away and squatted by the rough wooden wall as Sabre and George went through Sam's pockets and made a small pitiful pile of all Sam's bits of treasures.

Sabre gathered them into a red bandanna and held them up.

'Not much to show for a lifetime's service.'

'What shall we do with them?'

'Give them to Jodie. After all, the boy was very close to him and there might be things he wants to keep.'

George gave Sabre a level glance.

'He's young. We can't keep him with us.'

Sabre nodded. 'A bit of a problem. He knows very little about us, but what he does know could be dangerous for us if he was questioned by the right people.'

'Besides being a danger to himself,' George said meaningfully. 'Whoever killed Sam could go after Jodie for the same reason!'

Sabre stared at him, suddenly gripped by an idea.

'Maybe that's the way to flush him out.'

'You mean set Jodie up as a sacrificial goat?'

Sabre shrugged. 'Whatever you call it, it could work.'

'I don't like it,' George objected. 'It's putting the boy's life at stake and we're the ones with the orders to flush the Judas out and execute him.'

'There's plenty of us to watch him twenty-four hours a day. He'd not be at risk.'

'I beg to differ. We didn't consider Sam was in any danger.'

'Because we weren't expecting it. This time it would be different.'

'I think we should go to the Paradise ranch and check it out and see what they're up to. If it was Waterford who killed Sam, he'll be long gone and the only clue we have is this Paradise place. Maybe we'll get lucky.'

'I think we'll let Johnny take a look around first and if he doesn't come up with anything, we'll take a look-see at this ranch.'

Meanwhile, while Johnny quietly slipped away, Sam was buried in the lonely village churchyard situated behind the white adobe church. Father Francis officiated and only Sabre and his men and Julio and Conchita were present.

Father Francis said a few words of comfort to Jodie when Sabre explained that Jodie had been closest to him, having served in the same regiment with Sam.

Father Francis watched them all leave the churchyard, his hair swept by a sudden cold wind. The priest shivered and quickly made his way to the church where he lit candles on the altar and knelt and prayed.

Johnny returned. He'd had no luck in finding news of a stranger. The only person to see what looked like a cleric astride a donkey and making for the village two days ago was a man of eighty who looked nearly blind. He gave a toothless grin and held out his hand to Johnny for payment. Johnny ignored it and rode away in disgust. It was probably the local white-eye priest going about his business, but peons were all the same, expecting payment for opening their mouths.

Sabre nodded. It would have to be the long ride to the Paradise ranch.

They cut across country, Johnny leading the way. Joshua came up behind, leading the two pack-horses. It would be his duty to make camp some distance from the ranch, for when they returned from their reconnaissance.

The going was tough as they penetrated the range of mountains and moved further into Mexico. There were few signs of habitation but in the far distance a curling wisp of smoke could be seen. Johnny pointed it out.

'Mescalero Indians making talk.'

The Judas Hunters

'Can you read what they say?' Sabre asked.

'Just gossip. Talking about crops and their chief's son's coming marriage ceremony. Asking if they have corn to spare for the feast afterwards.' Johnny gave one of his rare smiles. 'All Indian fathers are like white fathers, they want to make a good show. It gives them prestige!'

They moved on and Johnny led them to a small basin of land surrounded by trees where they left Joshua to make camp and have food ready for them on their return.

They pressed on and even Carla was eager to see this ranch called Paradise. Johnny became ever more cautious now and twice pointed upwards and perched on rocks were guards sitting idly smoking with their rifles held loosely on their knees. It was plain they didn't expect trouble. As look-outs, they were just there for the merest off-chance and both men were bored and counting the hours for when their shift would be over.

At last Johnny thought it was time to tether the horses and go forward on foot to the place he'd found to look down and spy on the ranch itself.

Sabre was amazed at the size and efficiency of the ranch. It was evidently owned by a wealthy Spanish *caballero* or a Mexican *ranchero* of considerable means. He gave a low whistle.

'Just look at those corrals! How many horses d'you think're down there?'

The Judas Hunters

George Lucas squinted as Sabre drew his binoculars from their case and swept them over the terrain.

'Two ... three hundred at a guess,' George opined.

'And there's some mighty fine-lookin' big-horned cattle on that far range,' Roscoe pointed out, while Sabre studied the barns and bunkhouse, trying to gauge just how many hands worked down there.

Carla was taken up with watching the house and envying the long white-painted front with its wide veranda and vines growing up around the upright poles holding up the veranda roof. There were also large red earthernware pots full of plants obviously well watered every day. It looked very much like there was a woman down there who loved her home. There were also two lines of washing flapping in the breeze in the yard behind: women's bloomers and petticoats along with men's longjohns and shirts.

Sabre passed the binoculars to George Lucas.

'What d'you think?'

He waited for George's opinion and idly looked about him. It was then he saw the look-out on the other side of the natural valley. The glint of binoculars gave him away and it was as if whoever was looking through them was focusing on them.

'Uh-huh!' he muttered. 'It looks like we might be in trouble!'

The Judas Hunters

But it was young Ned who spotted the man on their side of the valley. He was above and well past them. Unknowingly, they had hunkered down below him under a overhang. The man moved and several small boulders rattled down the incline. Johnny, who'd slipped away, silently appeared.

'The look-out above us is signalling to the man on the other side. There's a wagon train coming into the valley. They're not interested in us. It's the wagon train.'

'How big is it?' Sabre asked sharply.

'Four wagons. Could be supplies for the ranch from Santa Monica, the nearest big town.'

Sabre nodded. 'It'll be interesting to see who brings the train in and what they're carrying.'

They waited more than three hours and watched a posse of riders go out to meet the incomers. Their stomachs rumbled and Carla cursed herself for not thinking of bringing hard rations for them all.

But the wait was worth it. They watched with interest as several crates of rifles were unloaded. George Lucas caught his breath when he looked through the binoculars and recognized the new Winchester repeating rifles. As the son of a part owner of a small-arms factory, he was expert at recognizing new models.

'Winchesters! They must be expecting trouble. Where the hell would they get them from?'

'Where else, from the bootleggers, no doubt,' answered Sabre cynically. 'Anything can be got at a price.'

But that wasn't all. As well as crates of ammunition, the supplies included hardware suitable for mining.

Sabre grabbed the glasses. 'Let's have a closer look. I think what they're unloading now is a pump.'

Sabre and George stared at each other.

'D'you think they're operating a mine around here?' George asked.

Sabre pursed his lips. 'Where's the nearest silver mine from here?'

George shrugged. 'It's got to be in this range of mountains somewhere.'

'I wonder if Waterford knew about this mine?' George shrugged and asked doubtfully, 'D'you think we're on the right track?'

'We've got no other leads. The sooner we catch one of them and find out who owns this ranch the better. Come on, all of you. Let's get back to camp and make some plans.'

They began to move cautiously away, crouching low, being careful not to disturb the foliage. Prying eyes could still be raking the landscape for intruders.

They were nearing their tethered horses when Jodie stepped out into the glade where they were. One of the horses nickered at their approach. It was as if it was a signal. A rifle shot spanged through the air and spent itself back amongst the trees. It missed Jodie's head by a finger-width. He went white and dropped to the ground.

Behind him Sabre dropped to his knees, while George Lucas dragged Carla down beside him. She and he, Roscoe and Ned all drew their guns and sent a fusillade into the bushes while Sabre dragged the exposed Jodie back towards them.

'Are you hurt, boy?' Sabre's question was terse.

Jodie, still shocked, just shook his head.

Then Sabre was blazing away with the others. The fire was being returned. There wasn't only one man out there, waiting for their return to their horses.

Johnny slipped away silently and quickly, to belly his way to the back of whoever was out there.

Sabre looked at their situation. They were caught in a trap. At the sides of them were steep crags which, if they'd attempted to climb them, would have had them exposed. At the back of them there would now be a bunch of marksmen closing in very shortly and then they could be picked off like tin cans at a village fête.

They still had not seen the enemy. He was firing blind and so were they. Bullets flew like angry hornets.

Then a loud voice hollered a warning.

'Come out now and hold your hands up or we fire the undergrowth and burn you out!'

The Judas Hunters

Sabre cursed. 'God damn you! Go to hell, whoever you are!'

'I'll ask you one more time. You've got a woman with you. D'you want to see her burn?'

'Now how the hell does he know that?' George Lucas asked worriedly.

'The same way someone knew about Sam, and then targeted Jodie first before we could take action!'

Sabre gritted his teeth and sent a burst of gunfire towards where the voice came from.

'Show yourself like a man,' he muttered as he reloaded. Beside him the others fired into the bushes, but there was no response.

Suddenly they smelled smoke wafting towards them and then the unmistakable roar of fire fast becoming out of control as it ate the dry grass and scrub. The ominous crackle turned into the savage menacing growl of a demon beast.

All around them small fires broke out as the wind became hot. Sparks flew all ways. They all felt the sting of tiny hot grits as the dry powdery earth was blown into the air.

Sabre stayed calm.

'Everyone, hunker down and retreat. We'll have to risk exposure and climb upwards. Maybe the smoke will screen us. We'll have to risk it.' He began coughing as a great cloud of hot smoke ballooned over them.

George held on to Carla and partly lifted and

partly carried her along, shielding her body from stray bullets. They came at intervals but now even those firing at them couldn't see what was going on.

Then Sabre suddenly felt his body plummet downwards. He tried to grab at the sides of the crevice, kicking and straining but there was nothing on which he could get a firm grip. All he felt was the jagged surface of rock.

Down he went and landed in a heap at the bottom. He looked upwards but there was only a mass of grey suddenly blocked by another body as it struggled and then come hurtling down. It was young Ned who got to his feet, choking and coughing.

They heard George yellng from the top.

'What happened down there? Are you all right?'

'Just a little shook up,' bawled back Sabre. 'Come on down and bring the others! This place might be our salvation. The fire can't get at us down here!'

There was a moment's silence.

'You're sure about that?' George was sounding desperate. 'There's no time to drag you both out.'

'I told you! Get everyone down here! That's an order! Dammit, man, don't you think I know what I'm doing?'

With those words another body came hurtling down and it was Jodie who rolled and gasped as he landed.

'Anything's better than being up there! The fire's getting closer!' He rubbed his already black-sooted eyes.

'Send Carla down next and we'll catch her,' yelled Sabre, bracing himself to break Carla's fall.

She was cool and sensible and jumped, pulling her legs up. She landed neatly in Sabre's arms.

'Right!' he shouted upwards. 'Roscoe and you, George, at the double!' They came down in quick succession.

They were just in time. Above them came the roar of the flames as the earth was scorched. There was a sensation of air being sucked out of the crevice; then it was gone as the flames travelled over where they had been minutes ago.

Gradually the smoke cleared. Blinking, they looked around at what seemed like a man-made shaft in the ground. What Sabre had thought was a natural crevice turned out to be a tunnel running along a stratum of soft rock.

Tell-tale signs of chipped rock made by pick-axes was evident as far as they could see from the opening. Beyond that was sheer blackness.

'What we do now, boss?' asked Roscoe, scratching his grey beard.

'Wait. Those bastards up top might be waiting for us. We'd be sitting ducks if we managed to climb out now.'

'*If* we can climb out,' George said softly.

'Yes, you've got a point there,' Sabre answered.

He peered upwards to see if there were any handholds. There seemed to be none. 'Appears to me whoever dug this here hole must have used a ladder to get up and down,' he observed abruptly.

'Then how do we get out? You got us in. Now you get us out!'

George's accusing glare masked a sudden fear of enclosed spaces. His breath was coming faster. He had the feeling he was smothering. He was panicking and knew it.

'We'll get out, no question about that,' Sabre answered, but he sounded more confident than he felt. 'Look, everyone take a rest while I go explore this place. Anyone got any lucifers?'

Roscoe and Jodie both had a box; they passed them over and Sabre braced himself for the task ahead.

He struck a light and peered down the tunnel. It led away, into the bowels of the earth, a snaking passage that seemed to go on for ever. Would it just go on to nowhere, or would there be another opening somewhere? It was to be a gamble not only with his own life but the lives of the others in his charge. They were his responsibility. George was right. He'd got them into this mess. He must get them out.

SIX

Rosa Mendez tended her husband. He was much the same as he ever was and she thanked the good Lord for that. He would never know about the circumstances in which they were living or her own infidelity.

It was no solace to know that what she did was to save herself, her husband and children, and Juanita, her housekeeper from certain death. She alone and her compliance with the hated *Americano*, kept them all alive, but for how long?

Rosa was sensible enough to know that when the time was right, the *Americano* would move on with his men after the small private silver mine petered out. Roberto had said many years ago that the lode would not last for ever and they must improve the ranch and prepare to go back to horse-breeding and cattle-raising. Roberto was old and wise, twenty-five years older than herself but a good husband and she'd been fortunate until just a little over six years ago when an *Americano* had ridden in. He'd stayed for the night and enjoyed their hospitality along with his platoon of men. He'd explained their presence in Mexico, for it was plain that they were *Americano* soldiers and that they were hunting Mexican bandits who'd been raiding up north across the Rio Grande and were wanted for robbery, murder and rape.

He'd so loved the locality and been so interested in listening to Roberto's account of the silver-mine, that they'd both been sorry to see the platoon mount up and ride away.

But all that had changed nearly three years ago when he'd returned with a bunch of cut-throats, taken over the ranch at gun-point and threatened them all with death if they didn't comply with his demands.

The shock of the raid had caused Roberto to have a stroke. He was paralysed down one side, his face was twisted and he could not speak. Gradually the light had gone out of his eyes and now he was a vegetable. Rosa had never loved him but he'd been a good husband and was the father of her two sons. She hated the *Americano* with a choking hate but hid it as best as she could.

Her hate was hard to hide when he took her in her own marriage-bed and she knew that if the opportunity arose and she had access to a knife she would kill him without compunction.

But he sensed her intention and seemed to get

an added thrill in making love to her and humiliating her. He even, on occasion, left a Bowie knife on the table by the bed, as if daring her to use it.

She knew however, that if she *did* kill him, his men would rape her one by one and then slit her throat. . . .

Now she waited, nervous and intense. He was due at any time. He came and went and never explained what he did when he was away from the ranch. He'd altered since those days when he'd come riding in, in a smart blue uniform, forage cap pulled forward to shade his eyes from the sun and his smooth good-looking face devoid of beard. Now he wore a full black beard, buckskins and scuffed boots and a greasy black broad-brimmed sombrero.

She knew he travelled far for his horse was always lathered. He would speak to the men, check the month's silver-ore and inspect its quality, arrange to pay the men through his *segundo* and then take her to bed. There it was as if all the animal in him was let loose. She dreaded his coming.

He was like a man thirsting in a desert.

He was due at any time, and now she sat by Roberto's bed and prayed. Oh, Mother of God, have pity on me! How much longer must I suffer in this way? Please, for my boys' sake, send me succour, and have mercy on me and all those in this house. Amen.

Tears were in her eyes as the two boys came to say goodnight.

They were beautiful boys, dark like her with liquid brown eyes that were too old for their ten and twelve years. They had seen and now knew so much, that sometimes she was ashamed of their gaze. She wondered what they thought of her in the privacy of their own minds, but she could not speak of her situation to such young boys.

'*Mamá mia*, we go to bed now,' said young Roberto, the elder of the two. She nodded and kissed them both.

The younger boy, Antonio, looked and saw her tears.

'*Mamá*, are you all right? Is *Padre* worse?'

She patted her son's head and ruffled his curly hair. How they had grown in the past year! Soon they would be men, if they lived long enough!

'No, *Padre* is fine.' She kissed him again, seeing the anxious look in his eyes. 'Go to bed, both of you and sleep well. I'll sit with him awhile, then I'll have an early night too.'

She watched them go with a heavy heart. She sighed. How much longer would this situation go on?

She heard the guard walk slowly along the veranda, his feet sounding hollow on the wooden planks. There was another guard at the back of the house. They worked twelve-hour shifts. The *estancia* was guarded night and day. She knew what would happen if she tried to harness up a buggy and drive out to their nearest town. She would never make it. She and her household were prisoners, watched at all times.

Now, all the men waited for the boss. There was a batch of silver-ore to load up and send under guard to Silver City where it was quietly disposed of at a price. The men too were getting edgy. Their wages were due and the boss was late.

Rupert Waterford eased himself. It had been a hard ride and he knew he was growing soft. His back and legs ached and he drew rein to look down at the expanse below. It always pleased him to stop and savour the view. Some day when the time was right, he would own all the land he could see and the sprawling *estancia* below, when the silver ran out, the men were paid off and it was safe to settle down into a new life.

As far as he was concerned, the past was finished. He'd had his revenge on the Union Army by fooling them and making a career for himself under the noses of the enemy. The massacre of his family by Union soldiers during an earlier uprising had been avenged by the massacre he'd masterminded at the battle of Black Horse Creek. He'd had no compunction then and very little now. He reckoned he was justified in his revenge.

Only occasionally, did his Catholic upbringing bring on nightmares of Hell and Retribution but a prayer at the right time eased his soul. Not that he thought of it as such. Usually on these journeys he fired himself up by thinking of Rosa Mendoza's body and what he would do to her in bed.

He knew her secret. She was beautiful or he would never have let her get away with it. It amused him to play her like a fish. Her demure downcast look, her seemingly eager compliance to sleep with him and even her supposed orgasms didn't fool him. She was a time-bomb, ready to pop, and it pleased him to see just how far he could go with her before he must silence her for good.

For he knew that for his own safety's sake, he must silence her, her stubborn husband who refused to die, her sons and the fat cook who, he suspected, from time to time put something in his food to turn his guts to water.

He made the last two miles in good time. The men were waiting in the bunkhouse as usual. The two wagons were loaded and waiting in the barn also as usual. He was satisfied. Luke, his *segundo* met him with a relieved grin.

'So you made it safely, boss. We was all sure beginnin' to worry, like.'

'Yeah, I'm late but got held up.' He dismounted, opened his saddle-bags and pulled out a couple of sacks which clinked. 'Here, count this lot and divide it out. Yours is in American dollars.'

'I don't know where you get all those piddlin' pesos from, boss. They're hell to count.'

Waterford grinned. 'You'd be surprised!' He didn't explain further. Luke took the heavy sacks and carried them into the bunkhouse. Waterford followed and nodded to the waiting men.

'Everything OK at the mine?'

'Yeah,' a big man responded. 'Much better since the new mining gear was delivered. Not one accident this month. But it's harder workin' underground. The lode's peterin' out. We'll have to use dynamite soon to locate a new seam.'

Waterford nodded. 'Maybe you and Sinclair should do some prospecting. There'll be a bonus for you both if you find a new seam.'

The man's face lit up.

'Gee, thanks, boss. There's some old Indian diggin's up the top of the valley we might look into. By the way, there were intruders a couple of nights ago, but we soon put paid to them. Snoopers, most like, but they'll not trouble us any more.'

Waterford frowned at the mention of intruders.

'Why? What happened?'

'Burnt 'em out! The sons of bitches wouldn't show theirselves when challenged. Reckoned they were up to no good. Probably heard rumours about the silver and were plannin' a raid. Anyhow we ordered 'em to come out with hands up and they refused and so we fired the grass and bush and expected the bastards to make a run for it.' He paused and glanced at his partner, Sinclair.

'Then what happened?'

The big man shrugged. 'They chose to stay where they was.'

'And?'

'The fire blazed up like the devil. The grass was dry and it took hold and it swept over where they were hidin'. I reckon they was choked with smoke before they could do anythin' about it.'

Waterford nodded, the momentary tension leaving him.

'You warned them. Serve the fools right. 'His voice was cool, indifferent. 'Anything else to report?'

'Nah ... only the men were gettin' restless, wantin' their pay. They got a powerful thirst on them. I've arranged for them all to take a night off and go to town and let off some steam. If it's all right by you, boss?'

'Yes, I've no objections as long as you leave some guards on duty. I take it the dogs are in good form?'

'Yes sir! A bit frisky-like. The handlers were havin' a bit of a job. A couple of bitches were in heat so they took the edge off the dogs and they're not so liable to take a bite out of anyone passin' by.' He grinned. 'Big Barney nearly got his nuts bit off last week. God help any stranger snoopin' around. They'd be in for a shock!'

The Judas Hunters

'Good! I hope they're still on a raw meat diet?'

'Yes sir, as you ordered. They're in tiptop condition.'

'So there's no reason why the men shouldn't have a night off occasionally. Keep 'em happy and they work better.'

'Yes sir! I'll tell 'em that you said they should have reg'lar drinkin' spells and of course, their chances to visit the womenfolk.'

'That goes without saying. Now, I'll just go on up to the *estancia*. Everything in order up there?'

'Yes, sir. There's a guard on the place at all times as you ordered. The *señora* is very quiet. Doesn't leave the *señor* much and the kids are no trouble.'

'Good. Any change in her way of life and I want to know about it. Right?'

'Yes sir!'

He watched curiously as Waterford left the bunkhouse and said softly to Sinclair,

'He's a cold bastard, is that one. I don't fancy the woman's chances if we don't find a fresh seam of silver. He'll up and off. I wonder what he does during the times he's absent? He must be living two lives. I'd like to follow him sometime when he leaves here!'

Sinclair shook his head warningly.

'You'd be playin' with fire, Bob. If he found out, you'd be dead meat. That kind has no loyalty to anyone but himself. Come on, get those bags opened out and let's count what he's brought and get the fellers paid before they go on strike.'

'They'll stop grumblin' when we tell 'em it's all set for tonight. It's a good job the son of a bitch came when he did or they might have wrecked the place and took off with the ore, and then you and me would have been up shit creek!'

They started on the task of checking names with hours of work before calling the men together for their monthly payout – which was more than a week late.

Rosa watched the dark figure of Waterford stride with purposeful steps across the yard towards the main house. Her impulse was to run away and hide. Her heart beat fast as she waited for the man who used her as a cheap whore.

At the first sight of him riding the trail towards the ranch she had called the fat cook and told her to take the boys and keep them busy in the vegetable plot. The woman had taken one look out of the window and gone without a word.

Now, Rosa waited. The decanters were filled with liquor, the stew was simmering on the stove, and hot water was bubbling away in a great iron pot. Whatever he needed could be had within minutes.

He stepped inside and paused in the doorway. He looked at her, savouring her fear. It pleased him to see her reaction to him. It felt good to have

The Judas Hunters

such domination over someone. It fed his self-esteem.

'Well now, you look prettier than ever! Don't stand there, come and kiss me and smile! Pretend you're pleased to see me!'

She moved across the room, raised her face to his and kissed him on the mouth.

'That's not much of a kiss! Put a bit more feeling into it!' She kissed him again, this time parting her lips so that his tongue could savour her sweetness.

His arm slipped about her, holding her in a cruel grip. He gave her a little shake. 'Come on, tell me, what have you been doing since I was here last? Not getting into mischief, I hope?'

She lowered her eyes to hide the hate she felt welling up in her.

'Just the usual things. Looking after Roberto and trying to teach the boys what they should be learning at school.'

He frowned.

'And is that all? You haven't been making eyes at any of the men? What about Bob and Sinclair?'

He felt her stiffen and thought to himself, if either of those bastards are two-timing me, I'll gut-shoot the snake in the grass.

She turned furious eyes to him.

'Because you use me, it doesn't mean I forget I'm a married woman! I rarely see your two overseers! I am no whore. . . .'

'Yes . . . yes . . .' he interrupted, 'we've had that argument before, but after all, you're a healthy young woman and your husband is . . . to put it tactfully, past it! Your lack of enthusiasm when I bed you, makes me think that someone else is taking the edge off your appetite!'

Her hand came up to strike him but he caught her hand and laughed, gripping her wrist so tight she gasped in pain.

'That's my girl! Full of spirit, but one of these days I'll tame you and you'll come crawling to me!'

With those words, he kicked the door closed behind him, swept her up in his arms and strode with her into her bedroom where he threw her on to the bed and flung himself on top of her.

Then, laughing, he ripped her bodice, exposing her breasts. Fumbling with his belt and flies, he reached up her skirt and took her savagely.

After it was over, he rolled on his back and let out a huge sigh of satisfaction. He wiped sweat from his brow.

'I've been wanting that,' he murmured. Then he looked at her, eyes narrowed. 'Now, fill the bath and before you do it, bring me the whiskey bottle, and then after my bath we'll eat and then . . .' he paused and tweaked one of her nipples, 'we'll start: all over again but take it nice and slow the next time!'

Bob and Sinclair watched Waterford stride purposefully to the *estancia* with mixed feelings.

They knew what was in his mind. Lucky bastard, they both thought and yet they despised him at the same time. If they allowed themselves to think about it, they felt both shame and sympathy for the woman and her family imprisoned in their own home because of this man's greed for silver.

The mine should have been their mine, the Mendoza mine and the workers should have been local peons so that all the local community should have prospered.

But they were greedy too and stifled such thoughts. The way they looked at the situation, the white men, flotsam and jetsam left over from the Civil War, had to survive somehow and most of them were wanted men back on American soil.

But they had no good reason to like the murdering colonel. He used them as they used him.

Bob looked at Sinclair.

'No good thinkin' of that sidewinder enjoyin' hisself with the woman. Just gives you an itch you can't scratch. Let's go and take a look-see at the old Indian shaft. We'll take a few sticks of dynamite along with a couple of lanterns and survey it proper. I've always wanted to see how far it went.'

'Might as well. If we find promisin' signs of good ore, it might please the boss and get us that bonus!'

They grinned at each other and made their way to the munitions dump where, amongst the crates of arms and ammunition were several cases of dynamite.

Bob surveyed the piled-up crates.

'He's got enough stuff here to carry on his own war. I wonder what he's got in mind?'

Soon, they were on their way, Sinclair leading a pack-mule with the equipment they would need and grub and bedrolls. If things got interesting they might stay out overnight.

The old cook watched them go. Bob had left him in charge. He was the only crew member he could trust. Cookie had the job of paying off the boys when they came for their grub.

Bob knew what he was doing. Cookie couldn't fork a horse and scarper with the payroll. He could hardly hoist himself on the crapper, his joints were too stiff. Cookie needed this job and he'd be a fool to foul up. The old man scratched his head and went back to cutting up beef for the pot. There'd be very few for supper that night. At least the leftovers would hash up for tomorrow.

Bob and Sinclair knew exactly where they were going. It was a location hidden by a stand of trees, amongst a litter of boulders. They'd found it once when they were looking for a calf. It could easily have been missed but the calf had been stuck in a crevice nearby. The big stone seemed loose and it had rolled away, leaving a gap as high as a crouching man.

Bob had reported it to Waterford on his next

The Judas Hunters

visit. Waterford had taken a look and noted signs of ancient digging inside. He'd questioned Roberto Mendoza about it in the days before the old man had had his seizure. The old man had shrugged.

'A Mescalero holy place. We leave it alone for good luck. Any who disturb those who rest there will die!'

Those words had put Bob, who was a little superstitious but wouldn't admit it, off from exploring any further and Waterford had just ignored the presence of the shaft until now.

Now the two men made camp in the hollow and decided there was plenty of time in which to start exploring that hole in the ground. They would eat and have themselves a drink or two before starting. Anyhow, by the look of the sky it might rain and they would be better off outside than in and maybe getting drowned out as God knew how a heavy rain might sweep through that underground passage.

They persuaded themselves that tomorrow would be a good time to start. . . .

Later, after two empty bottles and half of another had gone down their throats, they slept, oblivious to a rising wind which mingled with their snores, or the silent figure who looked around their camp, taking note of the pickaxes, the mining instruments and the torches. He extracted one of the paraffin-soaked brands and hesitated over the dynamite; then decided to take the lot.

He padded back to the sleeping men. For a moment he looked down at them; then his knife glinted in the faint light from the moon and blood poured from two throats that showed like obscene red lips. Neither man had stirred. He looked at them pitilessly and then left as silently as he'd come.

Johnny Eagle Eye had observed from a distance the attack on Sabre Wilde, had watched with horror as the fire raged across the earth, feeding on dry grass and scrub. There had been no chance of helping his comrades.

But Johnny had remembered old tales told by wandering story-tellers about the ancient sites in Mexico, of rituals only remembered by the old shamans.

He'd seen the desolation, the stark charred earth smouldering as embers still hot sparked and started new small fires that grew with the wind and then died.

He also remembered that most inlets had outlets too. No Indian forted up without an escape route. It would be the same with holy places. Even the modern white man, digging shafts for gold and silver, had outlets for fear of underground lakes and streams gushing unexpectedly.

After much patient exploration Johnny had found the peculiar boulder that seemed to stand out from the rest. It rolled easily to one side. It was as if that stone had been chosen for its balance.

The air inside was fetid and smelled of fungus. Water dripped somewhere, perhaps seepage from recent rains. He lit the oil-soaked brand and held it up. In the flickering light he saw that he was standing at the head of a tunnel that shafted steeply down into the bowels of the earth.

The interesting thing was that the air, although stale, was breatheable. This, Johnny reasoned, meant that there was at least a chimney if not an opening somewhere at the end of this tunnel.

He moved carefully, wary of snakes or other dangers. He moved foot by foot, the torch casting its light on the rock face. He saw carvings and paintings but had no time to stop and examine them. He wanted to find out whether his gut feeling was really telling him something or whether it was wishful thinking.

Were his comrades all dead, killed in the fire or had they somehow survived? All he knew was that he must search for them, to ease the guilt he'd felt because he'd not been able to help defend them.

SEVEN

Sabre inched his way along the passage in Stygian darkness, hands outstretched before him. Every now and again he stopped and lit a lucifer and took a good look ahead and at the ground before him, moving quickly until the lucifer fizzled out.

It seemed an agonizingly long time and there seemed to be no way out, but he took heart because unless it was his imagination there was a faint draught in the passage.

Suddenly his questing fingers found only space. The passage wall was gone. He stood still assuming that the passage must have widened into a chamber.

It was important to stand with his back to the way he had come. He must not get confused for there might be other entrances to the chamber.

He struck a light. One box of lucifers had been used and he was on his second box which was not full. He had to decide soon if he should go on or return to the others. He was sweating although it was cold and damp as a tomb in this place.

There was a rising panic in him that he had never experienced before when facing danger. But this wasn't the kind of danger he was used to. He wished he'd a torch of some kind. He cursed the men who had attacked them and put them in this situation.

He gritted his teeth. He must go on. Counting the lucifers in the darkness, he divided them and put half into the first empty box. He would use up one box after he got his bearings.

He lit the first lucifer and saw that he was indeed in a chamber which was highly decorated. He saw the opening and figured to follow the passage until the lucifers in the first box were done. Then he would have to admit defeat if there was no sign of an opening. He would light his way back to the chamber and then feel his way back to the others.

To be safe, he picked up several pieces of rock and piled them in front of the first opening. At least there would be no mistake about how he should return.

Then blindly he set off again, attracted by the draught. Surely it was stronger now and the air seemed fresher, or was that just his wishful thinking?

He was coming to the last few lucifers when he

The Judas Hunters

was sure the darkness was lifting. He put a hand up to his eyes and he saw its outline. Yes! There was light filtering ahead!

He stopped to take some deep breaths of air and the faint glow seemed to flicker. He stood still and he could swear that the light moved.

He must be hallucinating, he thought. Maybe it wasn't fresh air he smelt but some kind of gas coming up from underground. But it wasn't some fanciful dream born of sheer desperation. The light *was* moving and moving fast!

Stunned, he watched it coming towards him. Then suddenly he was galvanized to action. If it was coming towards him then someone was bringing it.

He moved silently and quickly to a jutting-out overhang and drew his Colt, nerves prickling. Then he drew a deep breath and shouted.

'Anyone there? I've got you covered!'

The light stopped and was shaded as if someone had put a hand out to shield the glow. Then a familiar voice answered back.

'Boss, is that you? This is Bronco Johnny . . . Johnny Eagle Eye, so don't let your trigger-finger slip!'

'Johnny!' For once Sabre Wilde fought an unaccustomed weakness as the tension drained out of him.

He heard soft running footsteps, smelled the faint scent of buffalo-fat that always hung around

Johnny, then firm hands were holding him as his head seemed to swim round and round.

'Boss, are you hurt?' A flask was thrust into Sabre's hand. He drank the potent Apache brew which hit his stomach in a swoosh. Then his head settled on his shoulders and the dizziness left him.

'No, Johnny, I'm all right and never so glad to see anyone in my life! Where did you spring from?'

'There's an opening and another chamber back yonder. I saw the flames engulf and reach out for you and I figured that as you didn't come running out of the fire and there was no sign of you, you just might have all found some tunnel. I reckoned if there was one, there would be a second escape hole. I found it and here I am. Where are the others?'

'Back there, waiting for me. I said I got them into this mess, it was up to me to get 'em out. I must admit, Johnny, I was never so scared in my life!'

Johnny looked at Sabre's drawn face, the scar on his cheek showing red through the beard, but it was the eyes that drew Johnny. They looked haunted.

'You rest yourself, boss, I'll go back and bring 'em out. I can move fast with this firebrand.'

Sabre sighed with relief. He hadn't relished the thought of blindly finding his way back.

'God bless you, Johnny. I'm ashamed to say it, but I'm nearly all in.'

The Judas Hunters

'Take another slug, boss, and you'll be fine when we come back. With that he was gone after thrusting his flask into Sabre's hand.

George Lucas was shivering as if he had the ague. Carla was tending to him. Roscoe with Ned and Jodie had gone back to the bottom of the hole and had examined the sides, Ned thinking that he might have a shot at climbing upwards again and rigging up some sort of rope-ladder to get them out.

All were uneasy, for the boss had been gone a long time and if anything had happened to him they could be facing a long agonizing death through starvation.

Carla alone refused to let her imagination run away with her. George, she knew was panicking because of the claustrophobic atmosphere, and tending him kept her cool. The more upset he became, the more practical she appeared.

Inside she was just as frightened as they were, but she believed in fate and if she was meant to die like an animal in the ground, so be it. She would be amongst friends.

It was Carla who saw the flaring torchlight. She screamed and the other men came running back to see what the danger was.

George, cowering on the ground, sat up, his eyes staring, as whoever was carrying the torch moved swiftly and surely along the black-as-night tunnel, sending ghostly rays of light ahead.

Then, as the figure came close, they saw the unmistakable silhouette of Johnny's scout-hat and the glow from the torch lit up his features like a carved teak totem.

'Johnny,' screamed Carla. Johnny gave an unaccustomed grin and waved the torch above his head.

Then Carla was stumbling towards him, laughing and crying at the same time. She flung her arms about him and kissed him on both cheeks. He stood like a wooden image and only his eyes gleamed to show his pleasure that the Mexican woman would greet him so.

He then told them that the boss was safe and waiting for them near to the escape opening. He led the way forward with them stumbling behind.

It was Roscoe who helped Carla. George hung back, now ashamed of his panic attack. Those hours in the darkness had been a time of self-discovery for him. He now knew that he was as vulnerable as any man; everyone had a weakness of some kind.

Sabre heard them coming long before he saw the first glow from the firebrand. He greeted them all with relief. He'd never appreciated before just how much of a family they were.

They all made their cautious way to the entrance. Everyone sighed with relief when they stepped outside and saw the night sky and the twinkling stars and a crescent moon.

Carla stretched and breathed deeply and in all their hearts they echoed her words.

'Thank God for open spaces! I'll say a prayer every night of my life after this and give thanks. I never want to go into a hole again until I go down in my box!'

Sabre looked about him.

'All seems quiet? Where are we?'

Johnny grinned. 'A stone's throw from the ranch. There were a couple of men camping out but they wont bother us none.' Sabre didn't ask for details. Then Johnny surprised him by bringing from under a flat stone a box. He set it at Sabre's feet.

'I thought these might be useful.' Sabre looked at him curiously. It wasn't often Johnny showed any emotion.

'What's inside?'

Johnny bent and opened the lid and Sabre gasped as he picked up several sticks of dynamite tied together with rope.

'Where in the world. . . ?'

'In the men's gear. Their camp is over yonder. Their horses are still tied up and there's a packhorse with mining tools. I think they were going to prospect down this shaft, but I beat 'em to it!'

'So! I think we better go see if there's any grub and then we'll make plans to look around the ranch and see what's going on. We can all do with a rest.'

They found the food Bob and Sinclair had brought with them. Johnny took his share and sat on a high ridge and kept a look-out as he ate.

Then, being the freshest amongst them, he announced that he was going to find his horse and ride back to their own camp. He would pick up Joshua and bring him back with their own horses, which would still be tied up where they had left them earlier.

He departed and Ned and Jodie who had suffered least, were detailed to stand watch while the others slept.

Johnny made good time, locating and taking the tethered horses with him back to their own camp. He expected Joshua to be around, a fire lit and maybe the smells of stew coming forth.

But there was no scent of stew and he sniffed no woodsmoke in his nostrils as he moved in closer. Suddenly his every nerve end twitched. Something was wrong.

Swiftly and silently he dismounted and led the horses into deep scrub. He tethered them and then, crouching low, moved cautiously forward, each foot coming down lightly so that he disturbed no stones or cracked no dry twigs littering the ground. He moved in a wide circle, gradually moving in and coming at last to the tracks he was looking for. He examined them closely. Six sets of hoofprints, one set of which dug deep, thereby denoting that one man was heavy-set.

He read the signs like a book. They had been there some time for the prints seemed to dance around some. Then he found the end of a cigarillo, nipped and not smoked to its end. They had decided to act.

So he wasn't surprised when he moved into the tiny clearing and there was no one to greet him. There was also no body, so they had taken Joshua to interrogate him. He wondered how long Joshua would last before talking.

He took a cursory glance at the camping gear and saw that it had all been picked over, examined and thrown down. No doubt on closer examination certain things would be missing.

He went back and untied the horses, then tied them Indian fashion from nose to tail. He was on his way back with the news of Joshua's kidnapping. There was no time to lose.

Sabre's reaction to Johnny's news brought forth a terrible anger.

'If that son of a bitch's tortured Joshua I'll kill him with a thousand cuts!' he raved and by dawn they were on their way down the valley towards the ranch.

They picked their way cautiously through the pines but could see the panoramic view below of house and buildings. There seemed to be very few men about. It was early and when the cook's triangle sounded for breakfast, they counted those who came from the bunkhouse.

Puzzled, Sabre turned to George Lucas.

'I thought Waterford had an army of men? I wonder what's happened?'

They watched a dark burly figure in wide-brimmed black Stetson open the door of the ranch house and stand on the veranda. He stretched as if greeting a new day. Then he strode over to the men's mess cabin.

'That could be Waterford. Look at the way those cowboys are greeting him.' They watched as several cowboys raised their hands to him as he passed.

Then Sabre frowned as a woman came through the screen door and stood watching from the veranda, her hand to her mouth and her shoulders bowed.

Waterford went into the mess and came back with a tin plate and a mug. Under his arm he clasped a bullwhip which trailed behind him.

Sabre tensed. He knew what a bullwhip could do. They were only used on the trail to control a herd, unless of course the whip was to be used as punishment on a man. . . .

Sabre swore. His teeth gritted.

'It looks to me as if we'll have to get down there fast!'

'Why, boss?' asked Jodie uncomprehendingly, as George gasped.

'Because it looks like Joshua's got a choice. Talk and get his breakfast or don't talk and get a load of bullwhip!' Sabre answered grimly.

There was a general muttering from the watchers.

'I'm the only one who can get close enough to get inside without being spotted,' volunteered Johnny. 'He's my blood brother. I go down and slit the colonel's throat!'

'No, wait!' Sabre put a hand out to detain him, for Johnny was for slipping away amidst the tall grasses to skirt around the back side of the barn. 'There's sure to be a guard with him.'

'So? I slit his throat before he knows I'm behind him,' Johnny replied, his eyes reproachful as if Sabre was doubting his skills.

'We're all going down. You, Johnny, can make for Joshua, free him while I tackle Waterford and the rest of you keep the rest of the pack back. For some reason the men are light on the ground. It would be a good time to finish what we came to do.'

They all nodded agreement.

Carla's eyes glistened. She was grateful that Sabre Wilde was treating her like one of the fighting team at last. She had shown her worth in the past. She eased the two Colts in her belt holsters. They were loaded and ready and she gripped the heavy Winchester with hands moist with excitement. She was ready.

Johnny went ahead, snaking through the scrub without disturbing a bird or small animal while the rest of them cautiously made their way down below.

It appeared that most of the men were still at breakfast which was a very serious meal as it set the team up for a strenuous day.

Smells of bacon and beef wafted to the oncoming group, making stomachs rumble, reminding them how long it was since they'd eaten a hot meal.

Sabre signed for Roscoe and Ned to burst into the dining-room while Jodie and Carla took the kitchen entrance. They would, with luck, hold the crew up and keep an eye on them. There was to be no shooting if possible. Their assignment was to take out Waterford, not massacre a bunch of innocent men.

George was to take the ranch house and round up whoever was inside.

That left Sabre to confront Waterford.

At a silent signal they all went to work. Sabre approached the door of the barn, hesitated and then booted in the flimsy door, ducking and rolling as he did so. Then he sprang up to dive into the shadows as a bullet spanged above his head.

Momentarily blinded by the dimness, Sabre dived deeper inside, leaping behind a stack of dried grass. Then his eyes cleared and he saw movement. It was Waterford, just a black silhouette. His arm was moving as the sinister whistle of the bullwhip shafted through the air.

It cut a swathe in the hay, sending the short dried fronds into the air as if they'd been lifted by a tornado. Out of the corner of his eye Sabre saw Joshua strung up like a side of beef, wrists bound, suspended from a hook. There were marks of the whip across his back and the dark dried crusted blood showed that the whipping had taken place sometime earlier, possibly the day or night before.

Sabre snapped off a shot which ploughed into the wood behind the shadowy figure, who was now bounding across towards a glassless window flanked by barred shutters.

Waterford paused just long enough to let off a couple of snap shots which went wild. While Sabre ducked, Waterford flung back the bars and dived head first out into the yard beyond.

The shots pierced piled bags of corn and Sabre was covered in both corn and a dustcloud that blinded him and made him cough.

'Goddammit!' he cursed as he struggled to free himself. Then he became aware of the Apache climbing in from a trap-door in the barn and dropping down lightly to free Joshua, whose head hung on his chest with eyes closed.

Dusting himself down, Sabre looked out of the open window but Waterford was gone. He heard

The Judas Hunters

faint gunshots coming from both the bunkhouse and the main house, but Sabre's first concern was Joshua.

Waterford could wait a little longer for his come-uppance.

Johnny lowered Joshua to the ground while Sabre offered him his flask and Johnny poured his potent brew down Joshua's throat. He coughed and gagged, shaking his head and groaning and then took several gulps of the nearly a hundred per cent alcohol.

Then he opened his eyes and grinned up at Johnny.

'I knew you'd come, brother, if I held out long enough.' He struggled to a sitting position.

Sabre looked him over. 'You feeling better, Joshua?'

'Yes, boss. I'll be on my hind legs in a few minutes. That bastard's a mean-arsed son of a bitch, but I'll live!'

'Good. Then I'll leave you to Johnny and go and see what's happening out yonder.'

He found two of the crew were shot, wounded but not killed. Roscoe and Ned were on top of the situation, with Carla and Jodie still watching the cook and his helper.

George was inside the main house. There had been some shots exchanged when Waterford had tried busting in. George grinned.

'I missed the bastard but gave him a nasty

shock. He came in the back door while the *señora* was making coffee. Tried to drag her out with him. She screamed out and I came running. He scarpered when I blazed away at him.' Then George Lucas looked puzzled. 'You know, I think I've seen him before . . . something about his bulk. I never got a good look at his face, but I've got this gut feeling I've come across him before.'

'Did you see which way he went?'

George shook his head. 'I had enough to do quietening the womenfolk and the kids. They all started yelling together. Quite off-putting it was.'

Sabre shook his head. 'We sure messed things up. Now we'll have to fan out and look for sign again.'

'Get Johnny on the trail. He'll soon track him down.'

'Yeah, thank God for Johnny. I'll just go and ask the *señora* a few questions. She might know where Waterford moseys off to.'

But Sabre got a surprise when Rosa Mendez told him that Waterford came and went at intervals with perhaps four or five weeks in-between visits. That he came and supervised the silver-mine, paid the men their dues, kept her and her family prisoner, meanwhile, and disappeared as silently as he arrived.

'Then you have no idea where he holes up?'

She shook her head. 'Nobody, not even the mine boss knows where he comes from or goes to.' She

The Judas Hunters

looked at him hopefully. 'Does this mean we're free now and he'll not come back?'

'I think you can rightly say that he'll not come back or if he does, we'll be ready for him. How many of the crew are loyal to you?'

'There's the cook and six Mexicans. All the rest belonged to him. All *Americanos*, they worked the mine in shifts.'

'Where are the men now?'

'Oh, they had time off to go to town. They'll be coming back soon. They stay overnight.' She blushed a little, embarrassed. 'They stay with the whores, y'know and get themselves drunk. Waterford allowed them to do that occasionally. Kept the men happy, he said.'

'And you, ma'am? What about you and your husband?'

She turned and pointed to a door leading from the main room.

'My husband is in there . . . permanently. He's old and had a stroke when the *Americano* raided us and took over the ranch. He's paralysed. . . .' She turned away, mopping her eyes with a handkerchief. 'He was a good man and doesn't deserve what's happened to him.'

Sabre put a hand on her shoulder. 'I'll see he's avenged, *señora*, never fear. Waterford's a wanted man and we'll get him in the end!'

Rosa Mendez accompanied Sabre and George to the veranda; Rosa was happier than she'd been for a long time. Sabre gave her a straight look.

'One of the first things we'll do, *señora*, is blow up your mine. Do you object to that? It's the only way to guarantee the miners won't come back with a scheme of their own.'

She nodded. 'We never needed the silver, anyway. As long as we can continue to breed horses and cattle, I don't think my boys would want to dig holes in the ground to grub up silver-ore! We want a quiet life here.'

'Good. Then we can get on and make plans.'

Rosa Mendez looked uneasy. 'There are two men in charge of the mine. One is Waterford's own foreman and the other is a mining expert. They might make trouble.'

George Lucas looked at Sabre meaningfully. They both remembered the two men Johnny had dispatched at the head of the escape tunnel.

'I don't think you should worry about them, *señora*. They've been taken care of.'

'Oh!' she exclaimed looking from one to the other. 'You mean. . . ?'

'Yes, ma'am. Taken care of . . . permanent.'

She was staring at them, her mouth a round O, when they were all distracted by whistling and catcalling coming faintly down the winding road from the valley towards the ranch.

They all looked to see what the commotion was about.

'It's the miners coming back from town,' Rosa

said quietly, looking at Sabre. 'They'll be easy to subdue. They usually have hangovers or are all tuckered-out with the women. All they want is grub and their bunks. Some of them will be sick as dogs. They're disgusting!'

'Good. Get yourself inside, ma'am and don't you or your family come out whatever happens!' With that he and George ran across the yard to where the others were holding up the crew.

Inside, the tension had mounted and Roscoe's reaction was to turn his gun on the door as they burst in. His gun hand lifted as he squeezed the trigger and the bullet pierced a wooden rafter.

'Jesus, boss! You shouldn't bust in like that! You might have got yourself killed!'

'The miners are coming in. Who's for the Mendezes?' He looked over at the men sitting idle at the tables. They all looked like regular *vaqueros* and Sabre remembered what Señora Mendez had said about her own men.

They all put up their hands.

'Now's the time to show the Mendezes some support. We'll surround the lot of them.' He turned to the cook – who stood apart from the others but was recognizable by his greasy apron. 'What do they do when they come back? Come straight in to eat?'

'*Si, señor*, or at least those who can eat. Others just want their bunks!'

'Right! Everyone out of sight. You, Cookie, stay

here and stir up your stew. The others hide in the bunkhouse and we'll take those who come in here. No shooting unless you have to. Savvy?'

They all nodded their heads but Sabre privately thought that some personal feuds might be settled.

The ranch crew members disappeared quickly through the far kitchen door, sneaked into the bunkhouse and hid themselves. Sabre's own men and Carla hid in walk-in cupboards, under tables and Sabre himself stood ready with weapons ready behind the door.

The clip-clop of hooves became stronger. Now they could hear a more menacing note and Sabre pulled the window curtain aside to get a quick look. It wasn't just a bunch of hung-over men coming back from a night of debauchery, it was something else. It sounded more like men intent upon further amusement, maybe even a lynching.

What he saw surprised him. In the midst of the riders was a dark figure that contrasted strangely with the miners.

Sabre blinked and looked closer. Surely the figure bound and gagged on horseback wasn't a priest? But his eyes weren't deceiving him. It was an old man, grey-haired and feeble-looking. He had lost his hat but there was no making a mistake for a silver cross hung around his neck. His clerical habit was torn and he looked as if he'd been badly used.

The Judas Hunters

Sabre watched as the bunch of men dismounted before the mess kitchen. One of them, who looked like a Swede, untied the cleric and dragged him from his horse. The old man promptly fell to his knees, but he was dragged upright and hauled into the mess, most of the newcomers following.

Sabre allowed those who were following to come in. The rest of the men were making for the bunkhouse. He heard muffled shots coming from the bunkhouse and as the bunch holding the old man turned to listen, he jumped out, firing a shot above their heads. At the same time, Sabre's own men came out shooting.

It was pandemonium as the men panicked. Only the big Swede managed to get off a shot. He cursed as he died with a bullet through his brain.

As he crashed against the wall, blood spouting from a crimsoning hole, the rest of the men sobered quickly and dropped their arms at Sabre's sharp command. While he and George and the others stood with guns at the ready, Carla moved around and gathered up the weapons, placing them well out of reach of any fool who might consider himself a hero.

'So? What have we here?' Sabre asked a down-at-heel individual who had caked blood on his cheek and looked as if he'd spent the night drinking and fighting.

The man eyed him sullenly, his hands held high. He spat at Sabre's feet.

'Who wants to know?' he asked belligerently. 'You're trespassin' and when the boss gets to hear of it, he'll come after you and carve you up into small pieces!'

Sabre laughed. 'Like hell he will! He's scarpered. Left you lot flat!'

The man looked astonished, and glanced at the others. They all looked worried.

'Take no notice of this bastard, Wilkie. He's bluffin'. The boss never leaves before sortin' out what has to be done. Why, there's a stack of silver to freight out yet!' The smaller, older man looked suspiciously at Sabre and the others. 'Is this what this is all about? You're hijackin' the silver? You've got a nerve bustin' in here! Wilkie's right, the boss won't rest until you're all six feet under!'

'We're not interested in the silver. We want your boss. Strikes me we can make a deal. Your lives and the silver providing someone tells us where your boss goes when he leaves here, then you all pack up and get to hell off this land.'

Wilkie and the old man looked blank as did the others. They shook their heads as Sabre looked at each in turn. His heart sank. It would be like looking for a particular flea on a dog. Mexico was a hell of a territory to comb for one man.

Then his eye lit on the prisoner who'd been standing propped up against a wall with his head hanging low. It was as if he was trying to make himself invisible.

'What about him? Why were you bringing him in a prisoner?'

Wilkie grinned showing twisted yellow teeth.

'Thought the boss should work him over. Talked some rubbish about gatherin' tithes, whatever they are. Somethin' to do with the Church. We reckoned he wanted a pay-off from the silver. Priests are noted for grindin' the poor down for the good of the Church. We was goin' to relieve him of any tithe, but the old fool got aggressive. Whoever heard of a priest carryin' a gun? Shot one of our fellers. Reckon he's no more a priest than I am!'

Sabre moved in front of the priest, stood with legs apart, his Colt pointing at the man's chest.

'Are you a priest?'

The old man raised his head and his old brown eyes were calm as he looked at Sabre. They were old and wise eyes who'd seen much suffering in a long lifetime.

'I'm a priest. Do you want me to recite the Lord's Prayer in Latin to prove it?'

Instinctively Sabre knew that this was indeed a genuine priest. He fingered his chin. He now had a problem. What to do with this bunch of men.

'No need for that, priest. I'll take your word for it.'

'Now see here. . . .' began Wilkie, incensed at Sabre's words, 'we know what he did! He shot a man. . . .'

'Probably with good cause! Even a priest must defend himself!'

Wilkie hard-eyed Sabre and spat.

'He shot Darkie just because the fool wanted his cross! He said no, it belonged to the Almighty and Darkie laughed and snatched at it sayin', the Almighty wasn't around to object and he wanted it. Then before we knew what was on, the bastard whipped a gun from his sleeve and shot Darkie, just like that!'

Sabre turned to the old man.

'Is this true?'

The priest bowed. 'No one steals from one of the Lord's servants, not this servant.' He raised his eyes heavenwards. 'The Lord will understand and forgive. I am under the jurisdiction of the Bishop of Mexico and travelling on his business. I am looking for Father Francis Octavius.'

Sabre looked surprised and a little puzzled.

'Didn't you go straight to Nuevo Cruz? Surely the Bishop would give you exact instructions where to go!'

For the first time, Sabre looked at him with suspicion. George motioned to him, coming close to whisper softly.

'Is it usual for a priest to carry a gun?'

Sabre pursed his lips. He turned to the priest.

'Maybe we should listen to you say the Lord's Prayer and maybe the prayer for the dying.... How about it, priest?'

'As you wish.' His right hand went into the pocket of his robe. There was a sudden movement as all guns were momentarily trained on him. He gave a half-smile. 'I only reach for my prayer book, for I might as well say prayers for you all before blessing you.'

Sabre felt a sense of shame but did not resist. They listened to the prayers and Sabre noted that not only were his own men moved but some of the miners as well.

Afterwards, he nodded. 'All right, priest, we believe you. Now you fellers can eat. Cookie here will dish out your grub but you're going to have to remain here. We can't risk any damnfool heroics! Jodie, get your ass over to the bunkhouse and get Señora Mendez's boys bring the rest of the fellers across here at the double!'

Jodie, thankful to be out of any trouble scuttled off and soon the cookhouse dining-tables were full of men waiting to be fed.

'Now, fellers, just take it easy. Eat and stay where you are for Señora Mendez's hired help have mighty sensitive trigger fingers!'

The seated men looked at the Mexican *vaqueros* who not only had their weapons ready but sported sharp-looking knives. They weren't hung-over enough not to be sensible.

Sabre motioned for his own men to leave with him, taking the priest with him. Outside, he surveyed the priest who showed no signs of relief

The Judas Hunters

or otherwise that he was away from his tormentors.

'What is your name, Father?'

'Vincente. I am attached to the Bishop's household and help with the accounts.'

'Oh? And what does that mean?'

'I look after the financial affairs of the rural villages. The tithes which are due, I record. Also the Church offerings. It has come to our notice that when His Holiness gave Father Francis Octavius the diocese of Nuevo Cruz certain monies should be paid twice a year. The covenant has not been honoured. Letters have been sent but not answered. I have been sent to get an explanation for the lapse and to present an account of what is owed.'

'Does that mean extra tithes from the villagers?'

Father Vincente bowed and clasped his hands.

'Indeed it does unless Father Francis has the money safe and is willing to pass it over into my care. There may be a good reason why the money has not been sent to Silver City. Maybe the good priest did not trust the transport available.'

'And you say he was not at Nuevo Cruz?'

The priest shook his head. 'I asked around the village for him. No one had seen him for some days but that was not unusual, his housekeeper reported. Sometimes he visits the sick in remote areas and arranges for services for the dead who live too far away to be buried in the churchyard.'

'Did they have any idea who he might be visiting?'

The priest shook his head.

'Not specifically. It was said he rides in the direction of Paradise Ranch sometimes and has been heard to joke that he never expected to live so near Paradise in this life. A man of humour, I think!'

'So that's why you were riding this way?'

'Yes, I thought I might meet him along the way and we could talk without being overheard. It's not the policy of the Church to let the parishioners know their business.'

'No hint of scandal amongst the clergy, eh?'

For the first time, Sabre saw the calm eyes flicker into anger. I touched him on a raw spot, Sabre thought. I wonder if there *is* a scandal? Surely Father Francis wasn't trying to rip off his Church and all it stood for? If it was true, then it was a dirty trick to rob the poor for he would know that it would be the villagers who would have to make up the deficit.

He studied the priest. Maybe this man would lead them not only to Father Francis but to the elusive Judas, Colonel Rupert Waterford. If Father Francis was crooked, then as birds of a feather got together, he *might* just be in contact with him. It was a wild, most ridiculous idea but the best he could come up with.

'I think, Father, that we should beg Señora Mendez to feed us and tend to your hurts and then after a good night's rest, we shall accompany you on your search for the good Father.'

'What about the men inside?' The priest nodded towards the cookhouse.

'Oh, I think we can leave them to the *vaqueros*. They have grudges to settle. We should not interfere.'

Father Vincente looked worried.

'I don't want them punished for my sake. I forgive them.'

'Never fear, Father, those *vaqueros* won't be thinking of you when they settle with them. I understand from the *señora* that they have all suffered much under the colonel's men.'

The priest crossed himself.

'God have mercy on them all!'

EIGHT

Rupert Waterford opened his eyes. It was early morning. Goddammit, he'd slept too long. He was cold and stiff. He'd dropped exhausted in the lee of an overhanging boulder after making his escape from the ranch. As a military man, he knew when to retreat. He was not overly endowed with courage. He'd always been better at giving orders and letting his men take the brunt of danger. Now he was on the run and he was dangerous.

But his mouth curved into a wolfish smile. Pity about the woman. He'd enjoyed her luscious body but there would be others. He would return to his safe bolthole and lay low for a while.

In the meanwhile, he would make new arrangements for that last consignment of silver-ore. Whatever happened, he was a very rich man.

He started when he heard the distant thunder of dynamite. He recognized the muffled roar for what it was. The sons of bitches had blown the

The Judas Hunters

mine! That meant that at no time in the future, when all this had died down, could he start again with a new crew. God blast them all to hell!

He was hungry and on foot. He'd never faced such a dilemma in his life. For a panicky moment he felt the terror that he usually had inspired in others. Then he got to his feet, relieved himself, started climbing . . . climbing to find his way into the pass that would head him back to his bolthole.

As he scrambled his way upwards, his eyes were everywhere. He looked back and saw far down in the valley a posse of men getting ready to ride.

He bared his teeth and spat.

'It'll take more than you bastards to stop me,' he muttered and went on climbing, breathing hard and suddenly breaking out in a sweat.

The idea had come to him like a bolt from the blue. Those men down in the valley were not interested in taking over the mine. They were not looking for silver, so why destroy the goose that laid the golden eggs? Were they there for another reason?

His mind spun. Had some of his brigade escaped the massacre and were now after him for revenge? How in hell would anyone know he was in Mexico?

He had to have a horse! He would kill for a horse!

The sun rose higher and higher and even in the

thin air of the mountains the sun beat heavily on his back, causing the sweat to run in rivulets. His thirst was hellish. He could feel his tongue swelling. He tried sucking a pebble but there was no saliva left in him.

His senses were reeling. If he didn't drink soon, he would be done for. Grimly, he bit his lips until he tasted blood. The pain kept him from sinking down to sleep. God, how he wanted to plunge into an ice-cold stream of mountain water. He raised bleary eyes to look around him for sign of water. There was none but he did see a faint wisp of smoke, or was it smoke? He wiped sweaty eyes and blinked, peering like some old half-blind man at the spectacle. It was smoke but whether it was coming from a white man's cabin or was the smoke of an Indian fire, his brain was too muzzy to decide.

He must force himself to lift each foot forward and blunder on. He walked towards the smoke which was coming from behind a ridge. Climbing the ridge took most of his strength. He collapsed at the top and lay like one dead, the ruthless sun burning down into his eyes.

Then turning on to his belly, he forced himself forward until he could look over the rim.

The sight put new strength into him. His cracked lips drew back in a smile that was a snarl. An old Mexican woman was pegging washing on a line and beside her was a crude well. He recognized it although it was only a rough ringed wall made of baked mud. But there was a pole with a bucket hanging from it.

His need for water almost made him faint.

He threw himself over the edge and rolled down over the loose stones and scrub until he reached the bottom, where he lay gasping.

The woman stared at him, petrified by the shock of seeing a stranger. An old man came out of the hut smoking a pipe.

'What's all the racket, Maria?'

The woman pointed. The old man strode across and stared down at Waterford, burnt, and blistered and gasping.

'Water!' he mouthed faintly and as the old man went to the well, he looked about him and saw the donkey. . . .

The old man heaved the wooden bucket over to Waterford, helped him rise and watched as he plunged his head into the brackish water. Waterford opened his mouth and let the blessed water engulf him. What relief!

He felt new strength surge through him. He stood upright and laughed, running his hands through his wet hair and all the while the old man and the woman watched.

Then, turning round, Waterford drew his gun and shot the old man and woman dead.

Breathing deeply, he went into the stinking hovel and found the source of the smoke. A blackened stewpan was on a trivet. Waterford took off the lid and stirred the mess with a ladle. It smelled good. Probably jackrabbit. He could smell herbs too and suddenly he was faint for food.

He found a bowl and filled it full. Then raking about he found a spoon and the coffee-pot still half full. He put it in the embers of the fire until the contents boiled again and then took it outside with a tin mug.

He couldn't stand the smell of the one small room. It was better to sit outside and smell the fresh air even though he could see the bodies lying quietly only feet away.

He enjoyed the food as he'd never enjoyed a meal so much before. Wiping his lips on the back of his hand, he poured more stew into a billie-can. He would eat again later. Then filling a canteen with water, he went over and untied the donkey. It was better than walking.

He felt his strength returning. By God, it had been close. He took a last look at the bodies. They would make good crow meat. He threw a leg over the donkey, which brayed in protest, kicked it in the ribs and it started off at a quick trot which slowed down to a reluctant walk. He was on his way.

Sabre Wilde ran his eyes over his men and Carla. He was concerned for Joshua, but he assured Sabre he could keep up.

The Judas Hunters

'All I want in my sights is that bastard! I want to see him dead!'

'You will, Joshua. If it's the last thing we do, we'll get him!'

Joshua nodded, satisfied. He had great faith in the boss. If he said he'd do a thing, he did it. No bother.

George Lucas joined the group with Roscoe. He looked pleased and was carrying what was left of the dynamite.

'You did a good job, George. You haven't lost your skill.'

George looked at Sabre and shrugged. 'When you grow up with an old man who runs a small arms factory you learn all about dynamite and gelignite as well as making bullets, goddamn!'

'So! We're ready to ride?'

They all turned as Rosa Mendez came on to the veranda to see them off. They'd eaten well, and all had food and water in their saddle-bags. Sabre touched his hat to her.

'Thank you for your hospitality, *señora*. I'm sorry it was necessary to blow the mine.'

She inclined her head.

'If it means no more take-over, *señor*, I'm glad. Now I shall be able to run the ranch in peace and look after my husband and family. Thank *you*. She smiled sadly. 'I want to thank you for letting those men go. I wanted no more killing. My own men will be enough to help me. I thank you for your humanity. God protect you and keep you!'

She turned abruptly, went inside and shut the door.

George said quietly to Sabre, 'We didn't make a mistake letting those men go?'

'No, we did the right thing. They won't be back. There's nothing now for them here. They'll be off to other mines, causing mayhem, but that's not our business. Let's ride!'

They moved out and Rosa watched them go with relief. Now they could get on with their lives. Her heart lifted. No more Waterford! Those men would hound him down. He'd not be back.

Sabre Wilde was frustrated and angry. The bastard, wherever he was, had eluded him and even Johnny had not come up with any clues. They had searched the foothills, growing weary and the old priest with them was beginning to flag but was still determined to stay with them, for this was strange country to him.

The days had passed and Sabre was in mind to return to Nuevo Cruz, get rid of Father Vincente and start again. Then Johnny appeared one morning after one of his forages and his face was grave.

'I think I have found signs of him, boss,' the Indian said without any other greeting. He squatted down by the fire and accepted a mug of coffee from Carla without looking at her. His eyes were fixed on Sabre. 'He climbed high into the mountains. That's why we lost him.'

'How do you reckon?'

'I lost his spoor when he hit the rocks. My mistake was to think he would make for a village. I was wrong. He climbed high. I think he was making for Devil's Pass.'

'So he was aiming for the other side of the mountain range.'

Johnny nodded. 'I found further proof. I came across a sheepherder's hut. The herder and his wife had been shot dead. Only a white man would kill like that and not bury his dead. The herder's donkey was missing.'

'How d'you know he had a donkey?'

Johnny rolled his eyes as if Sabre was asking a stupid question.

'A sheepherder would have to have means of transport up in the mountains and what better than a donkey? Besides, the panniers were still laid in the corral. I used them to bury the two bodies and then laid stones on top of them like you white people do.'

'Good. So he was riding a donkey. Where would he go from there?'

Johnny lifted his arms and shook his head.

'There are many trails he could follow once out of the mountains. He could pass through Nuevo Cruz without question or any other village he pleased.'

The Judas Hunters

'Then I think we should go back to Nuevo Cruz and ask around and see if any strangers have been in the village lately. Maybe he would be bold enough to call at the inn.'

It took them another day's riding to reach Nuevo Cruz and as they entered the village they heard the church bell tolling.

'Seems it might be Sunday,' Sabre muttered and old Father Vincente, who rode beside him, crossed himself.

'God forgive me! I have no idea what day it is!'

'No matter, Father. He will understand. At least now you will be able to rest and gain new strength and Father Francis will surely give you food and shelter and you can complete your business with him.'

They rode on, spread out and trotting slowly along the main street.

In the distance they saw the villagers streaming out of church, Father Francis at the church steps shaking hands and smiling. It looked as if he'd had a good turn-out, Sabre thought absently. At least the elusive priest was back at home from his round of sick-visiting.

They drew nearer, then Sabre heard a gasp just behind him. He half turned to see what was the matter.

He saw Father Vincente staring hard at the priest who was now looking up at the newcomers.

'What's the matter, Father?'

'That's . . . that's not Father Francis Octavius!'

Sabre darted him a glance, shock and something else clutching his heart.

'Are you sure?'

'Of course I'm sure! I met him at the Bishop's Palace when he got his orders from His Holiness. I was the one who drafted out the contract about the tithes! No wonder the first messenger we sent never came back! That man is an impostor!'

Roscoe moved closer to the priest, hearing the words. He was about to advise the old man to drop back when the man standing at the church steps saw the old priest and all of them saw the benign expression turn to cold wary anger.

Then, as if to confirm Father Vincente's words, a hand came up holding a gun and his aim was for the priest. The gun went off, and Roscoe, who'd shoved the priest from his horse, took the bullet in his shoulder.

Then it was pandemonium. Sabre's gun cracked and the bullet ploughed into the oaken door just as it slammed. The sham priest was locked inside, while the riders' horses plunged in response to the racket.

Sabre cursed and yelled to the others to surround the church and guard the entrances. Shocked, the old priest and Carla tended to Roscoe and lifted and half dragged him into the shade of a yew tree.

Sabre tried the oak door but it was locked. He

looked upwards thinking to scale the roof, for the windows were too narrow for a man to climb through; his mind was working furiously.

So the Judas bastard had taken the place of the new priest who'd been due to take over the parish of Nuevo Cruz and had taken in the entire village!

He turned to Jodie.

'Go tell the innkeeper and get him to organize all the fit men of the village. Tell him we've found the rat we were looking for!'

The boy wheeled his horse and cantered down the village street while Sabre decided what to do. First he must give the man the chance to come out and give himself up. That was the army way. He hoped he wouldn't take the offer.

'Colonel Waterford, can you hear me?' he bellowed, facing the church tower.

Far above, a small window opened and he could see a man's face. So the rat hadn't an escape hole he could climb into.

'I hear you. But you'll never catch me alive!'

'Then we'll take you dead!'

'Not if I know it! Why are you after me? Are you wanting silver? I can give you all you ever dreamed about. What about it?'

Sabre laughed and the sound was menacing to the man above.

'You can't persuade me that way, Colonel.'

'Does this persuade you then?' A quick movement made Sabre duck instinctively as a shot buzzed past where his head had been.

'Right, you stinking load of pig-shit, I'm coming up to get you!' He heard the colonel's laughter as he slammed the window shut.

Julio came at the double with more than a dozen men in their prime. His eyes wide, he'd heard a version of the disturbance from some of the villagers who'd witnessed their priest turning a gun on another priest.

He listened briefly as Sabre explained the situation and his anger mounted when he thought how he and the villagers had been taken in by the impostor and of the hard-earned *dinero* they'd given him.

Now his men were ordered to join the rest of Sabre's men in surrounding the two doors at the back of the church. He also reckoned there was a way out of the church that connected with the priest's house.

'Take me there,' said Sabre grimly. 'If he thinks he can escape that way I want to be ready for him.'

'If we catch him first,' Julio said, eyes flashing, 'we'll lynch him, the dirty slime-eating *diablo!*'

They broke into the priest house, where George Lucas rummaged around and found the colonel's own clothes, a quantity of silver and American dollars and several papers all carelessly bundled into a cupboard. A quick look revealed letters from the Bishop of Silver City berating Father

Francis Octavius for not keeping to their private bargain pertaining to the tithe money. These letters had been screwed into a ball and tossed on one side as if not important.

Julio showed Sabre the small door in the earth-floored cellar which housed the priest's collection of bottles. It seemed that the priests of Nuevo Cruz always lived well.

Then Sabre opened the door and looked into the earthy-smelling cold black interior. Inwardly he exulted. Now they would corner the bastard, do what they'd come all this way to do and then the job would be finished. They could all go home.

George peered behind him, a newly lit torch in his hand. Sabre turned sharply on him.

'Put it out! He'll see us coming and we'll be dead ducks.'

'But. . . .'

'Do as I say! You can bring it with you and use it as a club but we'll feel our way. If he can find his way through this passage, we can!'

Reluctantly George dowsed the flame but made sure he had lucifers in his pocket. Then gripping the torch in his left hand he felt for his Colt and eased it in his holster.

'All right, Sabre, what are we waiting for?'

They both moved into the dank tunnel, Sabre leading, feeling his way along the wall as he carefully put one foot in front of the other.

The way seemed endless. George was sweating

despite the cold. All kinds of images came into his mind, all connected with being buried alive. His nerves were jumping.

'How much longer,' he breathed in Sabre's ear.

'How the hell do I know?' Sabre snapped back, betraying his own tension.

Then suddenly Sabre could no longer feel the wall. It stopped abruptly and he stopped and swore.

'What's the matter?' whispered George.

'Shut up! I'm listening!'

George could only hear the beat of his heart. If he didn't get out of this hell-hole soon, he would scream. At that moment he realized something about himself. He was just as weak and vulnerable as any of the soldiers under his command in the past whom he'd accused of cowardice. It humbled him but didn't make him feel any better.

Sabre swore again. 'Oh, Christ, I'll have to take a chance and light a match and see where we are.'

'Then hurry up. I can't stop shivering.'

The match flared and they took a quick look around. They were in a charnel house and on all sides were stacked gleaming white bones. . . .

'Holy Mother of God!' George spluttered. 'We must be under the church!'

'Where the hell else would you expect us to be?'

The flame sputtered and died but not before Sabre had marked the exit straight ahead. Ten paces forward and they would be at the opening.

The Judas Hunters

He moved fast, George stumbling to keep up. He felt George's hand grasping his belt.

Sabre's seeking hand found the corner of the wall and then found by stubbing his toe that they were at the foot of some stone stairs.

'Easy, George. Mind your feet. We're on the way up.' He took the steps at a run. He heard George puffing behind.

His fingers encountered wood and he knew they would now be in the church. It was time to be cautious.

He groped for a handle, found it and turned it slowly. It gave and the door creaked. He held his breath but there was no sound. He opened the door a crack and saw the dimness. At least light was coming from somewhere. Then drawing his gun he swung the door wide and found himself in a cellar. The light was coming from a high-up grille as if the cellar was only partly underground.

But they were alone. Waterford was either still in the tower or else he'd been long gone.

Tension left Sabre as he made for the wooden stairs leading upwards. What the hell, whatever happened was meant to happen, he was a believer in fate. If it was his time to die, then so be it. He would have died doing his duty for the President.

He ran up the stairs and burst through the door ahead, gun at the ready. If he had to die then he'd sure take the damned traitor with him!

'My God, Sabre!' he heard George yelling, but

suddenly Sabre was all-fired for action. To hell with dithering around. He wanted action!

And he got it.

There was an ear-splitting explosion, as if an angry hornet had zipped past his ear. So the bastard had been waiting.

He ducked and dived, spitting out bullets as he hurled himself into the church. He heard footsteps retreating towards the altar.

Split-second reasoning made him realize that if he ran down the main aisle he'd be a target the colonel couldn't miss. He heard George coming up fast behind him.

'Get down!' he bawled and leapt sideways, crouching low so that he was covered by wooden benches, which had low backs. He thanked God for Nuevo Cruz being a wealthy church and not one that could only afford plank benches. Now he had cover.

Then he was darting forward, pausing to fire a shot and counting Waterford's answering fire. Maybe the Judas swine would run out of ammunition. But the slugs kept coming. The slimeball must be armed to the teeth.

George, grasping the situation, eased his way around the other side of the church. He hadn't fired a shot as yet. Let the black-hearted devil think that his only danger was Sabre. He waited, club in hand and gun at the ready.

He saw Sabre's shots hit the statue of the

Virgin, chipping off lumps of plaster. He saw Waterford as a looming black shadow appearing at intervals. He moved closer. Maybe he would get in a killing shot of his own....

Suddenly he heard Sabre's gun clicking on uselessly. Waterford had outfoxed him. Then the sound of a gun being thrown on to the stone floor of the church. It was time to move in.

Waterford laughed. 'So it's between you and me, Sabre Wilde. Oh, yes, I've known who you are for a long time, but not why you've come after me. After all, you're a turncoat. You betrayed the Union army just like me. Why not team up together? Or is it just the treasure buried here in this church that you're after? I could give it to you.'

There was silence as Sabre realized the significance of what the man had just said. He heard Waterford laugh again, mockingly, as if he'd known he'd touched a nerve. All men were avaricious in his estimation. He went on talking as if he had to tell someone of his phenomenal luck. He didn't wait for Sabre to explain why he was coming after him. Waterford thought he knew the answer.

'You want to know why I became Father Francis?'

'If you want to tell me.'

'It was after the battle of Black Horse Creek. I had to get away.'

'Why did you do what you did?'

'Why dwell on that?' Waterford answered impatiently. That is in the past.'

'But why?'

'The Union Army killed my family when I was a boy. I determined to make a career in that army and, when the time was right, have my revenge. Wouldn't you have done the same? But as I say, all that is in the past. What I did, was done. I could start again. God sent me Father Francis, riding his mule along the road, and so we travelled together. He told me he was the new priest making his way to Nuevo Cruz and he was sure of a warm welcome as they'd been without a priest for six months. It was too good a chance to miss. I could step into a new role. Survival is the name of the game, don't you agree?'

'Survival, yes, but not killing a priest!'

Sabre heard Waterford sigh. 'It was the only way.'

'And you killed the bishop's messenger.' It was a statement not a question.

'Yes, one more killing. What was one more after so many?'

'What about the treasure?' Sabre heard the colonel laugh.

'Now we get down to what's really important. Yes?'

'You might say that.'

'I came on it by chance. There is a safe in the

The Judas Hunters

church house which holds the village tithe money. There I found a key and wondered about it as there was no sign of a lock in the house. I found it here in the church behind the altar. There are church candlesticks and crosses and all manner of statues and gold coins in that place, enough to build every family in the village a new adobe house! Enough church vestments to make everyone rich! We could share it all and go on our way rich men. What about it?'

'The answer's no. I didn't come for loot.'

'Then what did you come for?'

'Your life!'

'But why?' Now there was a quiver in the man's voice. The arrogance was fast dwindling away. So much for a brave colonel of the Union Army, thought Sabre contemptuously.

'Because the President himself ordered it, and I work for the President.'

'You work for the President?' The words were whispered in a kind of horror.

'Yes. There's no escape, Colonel Waterford. It's over!'

'By God, it's not, damn you!' Suddenly the black shadow that was Waterford, launched himself into the air, Colt clicking uselessly. Sabre felt the impact of the gun on his cheek, knocking him backwards.

He felt the weight of the colonel land on him and he fought to keep Waterford's hands from squeezing his throat and cutting off his breathing.

His hand clawed the colonel, who fought like a maniac. They rolled over and over, hampered by the benches. Then they rolled clear and they were biting and gouging each other in front of the altar. George leapt the benches and crouched, ready to fire at the colonel if he got a split-second opportunity.

Twice George aimed at the colonel's head but the man dived and rolled as Sabre came up fighting. Both men were cut about the head and blood desecrated the foot of the altar.

George cursed and wielded his torch, using it as a club but missed the colonel and nearly brained Sabre. He cursed again and stood back, breathing heavily, waiting.

Then Sabre was under Waterford, legs kicking, each man locked in a death grip around each other's neck. Sabre twisted and turned and was uppermost when Waterford made a mighty heave and bounced Sabre over his head. He crashed against the lectern and lay for a moment half dazed.

Waterford struggled to his feet as George came at him with the torch and aimed for his head. Waterford saw it coming, leapt back and collided with the splintered statue.

Then, for George, all seemed to happen in slow motion. The statue toppled and George gasped and jumped backwards. He watched the heavy wooden statue come down, knocking Waterford to the ground. Waterford never saw it coming or knew what hit him. It broke his neck and he lay under it with arms stretched wide, his eyes wide open in surprise. He was quite dead.

George staggered forward, stunned and helped Sabre to his feet.

'What the hell happened?'

George just pointed to the Virgin.

'She took it into her head to intervene. Neither of us killed him.'

Sabre grunted. 'Remind me to thank her sometime. In the meanwhile, let's get out of here!'

He strode down the length of the church without looking back, then opened the double doors with a flourish. Outside, stood a crowd, Roscoe and Carla and the rest of them waiting and watching.

Carla's relief was evident; tears in her eyes, she flung her arms about Sabre and kissed him. She ignored George standing close behind him, who watched stony-faced.

'Thank God, you're safe!' she burst out. 'We heard the firing and knew you'd cornered him but we couldn't get inside, the door was locked.'

Sabre looked uncomfortable and unloosened her arms about him.

'Watch yourself, Carla. Don't go all female now it's all over! Remember you're a member of the team!'

The Judas Hunters

She fell back, rebuffed. 'I'm sorry. I got carried away.'

George stepped forward. 'I'm still alive, Carla!'

'So? What about it?' She turned away, sulky and brooding. When would Sabre Wilde really take a look at her? And more important when would he realize he needed her, not for her courage in a crisis but as a woman?

She felt sick. She could kill him sometimes. But there were times when she would have lain down in the mud and let him walk all over her.

She sighed. She must have patience. Some day. . . .

They were ready now to leave Nuevo Cruz. Their mission was completed. The Judas had been found and was no more. They could report back to General Fothergill and with luck return to their hideout and relax.

Sabre reached down and shook Julio by the hand.

'*Adios, señor*,' the bartender said. 'If you come this way again, there will be free drinks and meals all round. We shall miss you.'

Sabre laughed. 'And we shall miss you and the *señora* too. Tell her we enjoyed her grub.' Then he became serious. 'You will guard the treasure well?'

'*Si, señor*. We shall wait for a new priest to come and then we shall explain that the treasure must be sold for the welfare of the whole village or else we shall hire a certain famous *Americano* outlaw called Sabre Wilde to come and fight for our rights. How's that, *señor*?'

'You're learning fast, Julio. You will hold him in the palm of your hand. Use your power wisely, my friend!'

Julio laughed and nodded, raising his hand and waving.

'I heed your words *señor*. Adios!'

Sabre Wilde took a last look around, then looked at his men and Carla. All were ready to ride. His eyes lingered on Roscoe with young Ned on one side of him and Jodie on the other. He looked old and worn and seemed still to be suffering from his wound.

Maybe it would be possible to persuade the old man that it was time to hang up his guns. He looked meditatively at Ned and Jodie. God knows he didn't want two young men to sacrifice their lives to do the President's bidding. Ned was devoted to Roscoe, regarded him as a father and Jodie had lost Sam Small. Maybe making a home for the two boys might persuade Roscoe to retire. He was entitled to a share of the government gold they had stashed away for the day when those who survived would need it to start a new life. Roscoe could buy a ranch and they could all live as a family.

They would talk about this once back in their hideout. But now, the important thing was leaving

The Judas Hunters

Mexico and heading for home.

He lifted a hand, the signal to ride. He dug his heels into his horse and the little cavalcade trotted out of Nuevo Cruz.

The assignment was over.